Mrs. Atkins

The Hermit

Vol. II

Mrs. Atkins

The Hermit
Vol. II

ISBN/EAN: 9783337048174

Printed in Europe, USA, Canada, Australia, Japan

Cover: Foto ©Andreas Hilbeck / pixelio.de

More available books at **www.hansebooks.com**

THE

HERMIT.

A NOVEL.

BY A ~~LADY.~~ Miss ATKINS.

IN TWO VOLUMES.

VOL. II.

LONDON:

Printed for H. Gardner, opposite St. Clement's
Church, Strand; and sold by J. Walter,
at Charing-Cross; and G. Pearch,
at No. 12, in Cheapside.

MDCCLXIX.

THE

HERMIT.

CHAP. XV.

" Y OU are not ignorant, my
" fair audience, of my fa-
" mily, fince it is the fame
" with this gentleman's, whofe fa-
" ther and myfelf were the only
" children our parents ever had."

VOL. II.   B   " MY

" MY brother being the eldeſt was
" brought up to no profeſſion; but I,
" who had nothing to expect but a mo-
" derate fortune, when about nineteen,
" my inclinations firſt conſulted, was
" ſettled in *London* with a merchant of
" great eminence.

" AFTER I had been with this good
" man upwards of three years, he not
" only gave his buſineſs, but alſo his
" only, his lovely, his moſt amiable
" daughter to me.—It is impoſſible
" (continued he) you can be a judge
" of the greatneſs of this laſt gift: you
" did not know my *Emily*.—Her
" beauty, though exquiſite, was the
" leaſt of her charms:—ſhe had a
" mind repleniſhed with every virtue;
" a diſpoſition ſo mild, ſo exalted, yet
" ſo ſweetly condeſcending, that I could
" dwell forever on her perfections.

" How

" How fupremely happy did the
" firft ten years after our marriage
" find us : each returning month haf-
" tened to me with fome new felicity.
" I will only here recount a few of thofe
" bleffings I then enjoyed :—riches
" fufficient to fatisfy the moft ambi-
" tious mind;—a wife on whom I
" doated;—children who early pro-
" mifed to be an honour and a com-
" fort to their parents.

" I HAD already two fons, and my
" *Emily* in a way to add to that num-
" ber, when clouds dark as night be-
" gan to obfcure all my brighter prof-
" pects. Their firft appearance was in
" the death of that worthy man who
" gave being to the object of my ten-
" dereft love.

B 2   " I WAS

" I WAS obliged to fupprefs what I
" felt on this occafion, and confole
" his afflicted daughter, whofe grief,
" though calm, I knew to be more def-
" tructive than if it had raged with
" violence: but foon, too foon, was
" the dear creature roufed from her
" lethargic forrow."

" IT was now my *Emily's* turn to
" difplay her foothing eloquence.—
" How did the fweet monitrefs expa-
" tiate on the inftability of fublunary
" enjoyments! how did fhe bring the
" death of her father to convince me,
" that I had not a greater right to com-
" plain at the hourly expected lofs of
" mine!

" THOUGH I knew her arguments
" to be founded on wifdom, I did
" not juft then feel all their energy.—
                              " Oppreffed

" Oppreffed with grief, I determined
" to fet out immediately for the
" *Grove*. A letter my brother fent
" by one of my father's fervants did
" not feem to hint fuch expedition
" was neceffary; at the fame time
" it informed me, the beft of parents
" was dangeroufly indifpofed.

" My wife could not be prevailed on
" to ftay behind.—Though I dreaded
" the confequence of fo long a journey
" to a perfon in her fituation, her im-
" portunities got the better of my fcru-
" ples. Wretched, unfortunate com-
" pliance !

" AFTER fpending an hour in my
" counting-houfe with my partner, on
" whom I had the greateft reliance, we
" ftepped into a chaife, taking with
" us our eldeft boy, a lovely child, a-

" bout

" bout feven years old. Oh heaven!
" how can I repeat what followed
" (exclaimed the good old man)! It
" unhinges my very nature! Yet I
" muſt, I will try to proceed!

" THIS moſt miſerable journey hap-
" pened in the winter, and at a time
" when the waters were fwoln by
" heavy falls of rain. — Within
" ten miles of the *Grove,* we were
" obliged to croſs a ſmall rivulet,
" which emptied itſelf into a large ri-
" ver; and juſt as we had entered it,
" the horſes taking fright turned the
" contrary way, carrying us in an in-
" ſtant down the horrid current. What
" a dreadful moment! Oh my dear
" wife! thy ſhrieks, my infant's ſcreams
" ſtill vibrate on my ear! But the
" cruel water bereft you of your
" voices!

" FROM

" FROM the inftant I perceived our
" danger, my fenfes became ftupified.
" Unluckily for me, by fome unfore-
" feen means the door of our finking
" carriage burft open, by which ac-
" cident my life was preferved.   I was
" driven on the fhore, from whence
" I was taken up and carried to a
" poor cottage, where the humanity of
" its inhabitants preferved a life which
" has been from that hour wretched.

" SOON as I could fpeak, without
" any recollection of what had hap-
" pened, I afked for my wife and
" child : but this happy infenfibility
" did not laft long; the words
" were fcarce paffed my lips when the
" door opened, and a number of peo-
" ple crouded in, fome of whom bore
" their breathlefs bodies.

B 4   " REASON

" REASON could not be expected to
" keep her feat after fo dreadful a
" fhock ; fhe kindly took her flight,
" and in her abfence I was unac-
" quainted with my extreme mifery.

" THE people at whofe houfe I was,
" finding by a letter in my pocket to
" what family I belonged, fent an
" account to my brother ; for my
" dear father was by this time num-
" bered amongft the bleffed."

" MY brother, too much engaged
" in fettling his affairs to come in per-
" fon, fent his fteward, a worthy
" good man, to whofe care and the
" fkill of an excellent phyfician I owe
" the recovery of my fenfes, after
" they had deferted me near three
" weeks.

" IN

" In the beginning of my delirium
" I could not be torn from my life-
" lefs *Emilia* and her fweet child, to
" whom I talked as if they were ftill
" living.

" Mr *Bending's* firft care was to get
" thefe melancholy objects removed to
" our family-vault; and in a month,
" though ftill extremely weak, my
" phyfician permitted me to be re-
" moved to the *Grove*, where I was
" received with every mark of affec-
" tion by my brother and fifter, both
" of whom had often been to vifit me
" at the cottage.

" Whatever tendernefs my bro-
" ther affumed on this occafion, time
" and experience has fince convinced
" me was but an appearance, though
" it then helped to fupport me under

" my

" my misfortunes.—His wife, the
" moſt amiable of women, was calcu-
" lated to drive melancholy from every
" breaſt where it had not taken a too
" deep root; but as that was the caſe
" with me, all her kind aſſiduities
" were beſtowed in vain.

" I took no ſort of ſatisfaction in
" any thing I ſaw or heard; all was
" alike indifferent. My mind, though
" it had attained ſomething that reſem-
" bled a calm, nevertheleſs felt inani-
" mate: the neareſt ſimilitude I can
" draw of myſelf is, a wretch beſotted
" with liquor, who ſees and hears his
" companions, but is diſabled from at-
" tending to their converſation, or
" joining in it.

" If I could be ſaid to take any de-
" gree of ſatisfaction, it was in the
                              " company

" company of my nephew, then about
" eight years old: his innocent prat-
" tle would oft remind me of my *Ed-*
" *ward*, to whom I was now impa-
" tient to return; but was obliged to
" defer my journey longer, as there
" were yet affairs to be fettled, in
" which my prefence would be ne-
" ceffary.

" DURING my refidence at the *Grove*
" I difcovered this retreat: its gloomy
" afpect pleafed me.. I could even at
" that time have fpent the remainder
" of my days in it, had not the
" thoughts of my dear boy forbad the
" defign, and fhewed me on his ac-
" count the neceffity I was under of
" returning to the world.

" IN the evening, when I came
" back to the *Grove*, I was juft about

" to recount to my brother what had
" detained me fo long, having fpent
" the whole day in viewing over this
" fubterraneous cavern, which I could
" then do without the affiftance of
" candles, as the door by which we
" entered, as well as that by which we
" left it, was a contrivance of my own,
" to make it the more concealed. But
" I break the thread of my narrative—
" I faid I was going to defcribe this
" rock to my brother, when I was
" prevented by a letter delivered at that
" inftant.

" THE alteration of my countenance,
" as I read it, made my brother afk if
" it contained any ill news.—I ought
" not (I replied) to think any thing
" a misfortune, after thofe dreadful
" ones I have lately experienced. Alas!
" I do not feel for myfelf, indeed I
" do

" do not; but O my child! my dear
" child! how will thy tender years
" be able to ſtruggle with adverſity!
" to be debarred, perhaps, the very
" neceſſaries of life, or, what is ſtill
" worſe, obliged for them to depend
" on the ſmiles of the Great.".

" A HINT of poverty drove every
" trace of regard from the face of my
" unkind brother. In the place of
" ſmiles and complacency, how cold,
" how icy the countenance he now
" aſſumed! Yet ſcarcely able to cre-
" dit what I ſaid, he aſked me why I
" talked in that unaccountable ſtrain.
" Have you not (cried he) large ſums
" in the Bank, beſides your ſtock in
" trade? Why, then, talk of depen-
" dance for your child?"

" A WEEK

"A week since (anſwered I) it was
"as you ſay; but my partner, who till
"now has ever bore the moſt honour-
"able character, throws aſide the
"maſk: he has not only drawn out
"all my monies, but called up many
"of my debts, with which booty he
"has left the kingdom."

"Drawn out your money! (cried
"he with redoubled emotions of diſ-
"appointment and ſurpriſe) how is
"that poſſible?"

"It was very poſſible (returned I).
"Thinking him honeſt, I put the
"weapon into his hand, with which
"he has ſtabbed me:—I left him in
"my abſence a power to manage even
"my private fortune."

"Then

" Then I suppofe, Sir (replied he,
" coldly), you are not to blame in
" this fine affair? Who but you would
" have trufted to appearances? My
" advice was never afked; fo you can-
" not expect, Sir, I will involve my-
" felf in your mifmanaged affairs.—
" Yet, if it will be of any real fer-
" vice, I am not againft advancing the
" five thoufand pounds left you by my
" father, though it is three months
" before you can otherwife demand
" it."

Here I muft beg leave to take my
readers' attention one moment from
the narrative, to acquaint them Mr.
Harry Gore had left the room whilft
the old gentleman was recounting the
melancholy death of his wife. This
he did to relieve his heart by a few
friendly drops, and to avoid hearing
" the

the unbrotherly treatment his uncle
experienced from a man whofe memory he could not but revere, having
ever fhewn himfelf a very indulgent
parent.   I know this interruption extremely *mal-à-propos*; for which reafon
I return to the Hermit's continuation
of his affecting ftory.

" The indignation (faid he) which
" I felt at this converfation is not to
" be expreffed.   I could hardly be-
" lieve fuch cutting taunts, fuch cruel
" reflections, could come from a bro-
" ther whofe love I never doubted. I
" looked at him as if I would have
" pierced his foul. I replied, " Doubt-
" lefs my misfortunes are fent me for
" wife ends; nay, I am convinced
" they are (added I) : For had my
" wife lived, I fhould have thought
" with pain of quitting a world where

" I

" I enjoyed fuch happinefs. The lofs
" of fortune fhews me people in a true
" light: Poverty is a touchftone to
" friendfhip."

" THIS touched his confcious bo-
" fom; and he returned, with a look
" of more rage than I can defcribe,
" You moralize, Sir, extremely well;
" though your laft expreffion might
" have been fpared. You have yet
" loft no friend; at leaft, I think I
" have fhewn myfelf one in the offer
" I have juft made you: But as to
" any farther involvements, take it
" how you pleafe, brother, I will
" avoid them."

" NOT to be warm on that ac-
" count, Sir (replied I), before Heaven
" I now proteft, you are the laft man
" I will apply to."

" MY

" My sister coming into the room
" prevented his answer; and when I
" told her I should set out for *London*
" early the next morning, she ap-
" peared surprized; but as her huf-
" band did not ask me to put off my
" journey, she supposed that particu-
" lar affairs required my presence, and
" only expressed her concern at my
" leaving them.

" The following day I left the
" *Grove*; and that same evening had
" the inexpressible pleasure to embrace
" my sweet *Edward*, whose innocent
" caresses made me forget half my
" sufferings.

" When I came to look into my
" affairs, I found them not quite so
" bad as I expected; and the five
" thousand pounds, which I would not
" receive

" receive till it became due, fet me
" once more in a flourifhing way.

" At the end of ten years I found
" myfelf poffeffed of twenty thoufand
" pounds. Though not in the leaft
" adequate to my former fortune, yet
" it made me happy, as it was very
" fufficient to place my dear fon
" above dependance; a ftate I always
" dreaded.

" I now refolved to retire from
" bufinefs, and only waited the arri-
" val of the *Weft-India* fleet, from
" which I had great dependance, to
" put my defign in execution: But
" here I again met with a new mif-
" fortune; the fhips which I expected
" were all loft in their paffage.

" My

" My creditors judging I could not
" support this second blow, took out
" againſt me a ſtatute of bankruptcy.
" My dear *Edward*, now fifteen,
" ſhewed on this occaſion a heroiſm
" far above his years: He never once
" repined; on the contrary, declared
" he felt no uneaſy thought but for
" his father. " You have educated
" me (ſaid this beſt of children) in a
" manner which will entitle me at
" leaſt to a genteel proviſion. Be-
" ſides, have you not often told me,
" God will never forſake thoſe who
" believe and rely on him? Why
" then, my deareſt Sir, would you
" think he will abandon us?"

" I DO not, my Love (I replied);
" he will, doubtleſs, protect thy inno-
" cence; and in thee I ſhall be re-
" warded for all my ſufferings."

　　　　　　　　　" AFTER

" AFTER two months my affairs
" being fettled, I regained my liberty;
" and my creditors, finding I had act-
" ed with the ftricteft honour, many
" of them offered to affift me, if I
" again would enter into trade : But
" this I declined, refolving no more to
" truft the property of others in a bark
" which Fortune fhewed a fettled re-
" folution to deftroy.

" EDWARD often wondered that
" his uncle had never offered me his
" affiftance, and ftrenuoufly defired I
" would either write, or permit him
" to go in perfon ; but I abfolutely re-
" fufed both, telling my fon, that,
" after his uncle's former ufage, and a
" neglect of fo many years, I could
" not think of putting it a fecond time
" in his power to infult me.

" NOT-

" NOTWITHSTANDING all I faid,
" he was determined on one trial,
" and fet out unknown to me; pre-
" tending he was going to vifit a
" Mr. *Elliott*, who was his fchool-
" fellow.

" KNOWING he had a great efteem
" for this young gentleman, it gave
" me pleafure to part with him: But
" inftead of going to *Reading*, he pro-
" ceeded immediately to the *Grove*.
" But oh, my God ! how was his du-
" tiful heart torn by the reception he
" there met ! Cold as winter's froft
" was this cruel brother to my fweet
" bloffom, fcarcely hearing him with
" common civility, abfolutely refufing
" to affift me. " I fuppofe, young
" man (faid he, with a fneer), your
" father did not acquaint you with the
" refo-

" refolution he formerly made, that I
" fhould be the laft perfon to whom
" he would apply ? "

" My fon, with refentment that
" fpoke more in his eyes than words,
" faid, " You are right, Sir; my father
" is ignorant of the ftep I have now
" taken. He too well knew your dif-
" pofition to think it would be of effi-
" cacy; but my inexperience in life
" made me fcarcely credit that a Chrif-
" tian, bound by every tie, divine or
" human, could fee a brother, that
" brother fo deferving, even in the
" jaws of ruin, and not reach out his
" hand to fave him. But my credu-
" lity is cured ; you have fhewn me
" there are fuch men. Adieu, Sir (to
" my brother). This is the laft time
" you fhall be troubled with the fight
" of

" of me." Saying which, he hurried
" to the door; nor did his uncle at-
" tempt to detain him.

CHAP. XVI.

" EDWARD, on his return to
" *London*, could not conceal
" the chagrin he felt at this cruel and
" inhoſpitable treatment; and, after
" many importunities, I wrung the ſe-
" cret from him.

" THOUGH this freſh inſtance of
" my brother's unkindneſs gave me a
" ſevere pang, yet to my ſon I made
" light of it, unwilling to add any
" concern of mine to what he already
" ſuffered.

" HE

" HE was now the only comfort I
" had left; of every other I was be-
" reft; yet ftill in him rich beyond
" my hopes. Such fenfe, fuch wif-
" dom, duty fo exemplary! But then
" to lofe him! Oh, it was too, too
" much! Yet let not a man, a liv-
" ing man complain: Rather let me
" fay with *Job, The Lord gave, and the*
" *Lord taketh away, and bleffed be the*
" *name of the Lord!*"

THIS ejaculation he pronounced
with ftreaming eyes, uplifted to Heaven. As for his fair auditors, it might
have been thought their tears flowed
from exhauftlefs fountains. But as I
doubt not many of my gentle readers
are bleffed with hearts equally fufcep-
tible, I fhall not take upon me to defcribe the tender fenfations of fuch

VOL. II.   C   minds

minds as can feel for the woes of others. As for thofe of a different complection, it is impoffible that even a *Shakefpeare*'s pen, or the pencil of a *Raphael*, fhould give them any conception of the fympathetic forrow which filled the breafts of *Maria* and *Lavinia.*

" I HAD ftill (continued Mr. *Gore)*
" one friend left, and not a fummer
" one, that leaves us as foon as
" bleak wind blow. This gentle-
" man had in my affluence been
" perfectly obliging, but never fhewed
" me any particular tendernefs, till I
" thought myfelf forfaken by the
" world. It was then he flew to me,
" and held out the balfam of friend-
" fhip: By him we were fupported in
" our blafted fortunes; my dear *Ed-*
. " *ward*

" *ward* looked on him as a fecond fa-
" ther, I as my preferving angel.

" ONE morning he came to us with
" a countenance more than ufually
" delighted, and fhaking me cordi-
" ally by the hand, he took that of
" my fon *Edward*, faying with a
" fmile, " I want to petition your
" father on an affair in which you muft
" ftand my advocate, or I fhall be
" apprehenfive of not fucceeding."

" WHAT an ungrateful creature do
" you think me, my friend (replied
" I) ! Sure there is nothing within my
" little power which you may not
" freely command. Tell me, I in-
" treat you, in what I can ferve the
" man on earth to whom I am moft
" obliged."

Nor

" Not a word of obligations (cried
" he), and I will satisfy you in what
" manner you may infinitely pleafe me.
" But forbear to interupt me till I have
" given reafons for what I am about
" to afk."

" I yesterday left you (purfued
" he) in order to attend a meeting at
" the *India-houfe*, when, without the
" leaft expectation of that honour, I
" was unanimoufly elected governor
" of *Bengal*, and defired to get my-
" felf ready with all poffible expedition
" for my embarkation. Now it in-
" ftantly occurred to me that I would
" folicit the company of my dear
" *Edward*."

" I turned pale, ftarted, and was
" going to interrupt him; but he
" prevented me by humoroufly put-
" ting

" ting his hand before my mouth. " I
" muft, I fee (faid he), remind you of
" your promife: I have not yet done.
" I know what I afk will, at firft,
" give you pain ; but on reflection you
" will find, that by going with me,
" he cannot fail of returning in a few
" years poffeffed of a fortune to fhine
" in that fphere to which his birth,
" fenfe, and fine accomplifhments en-
" title him."

" EDWARD's face was vermilioned
" to hear thofe praifes, though juftly
" beftowed upon him.

" WELL, (faid our friend) I have
" but one thing more to add: You
" know I am now a batchelor, and if
" I hold in my prefent mind fhall pro-
" bably continue one; but this I do
" not pofitively fay will be the cafe.

C 3 " Yet

" Yet, fuppofing it fo, I fhall look on
" *Edward* as my fon, and as fuch pro-
" vide for him at my death.——Now
" for this reafon I think it will be for his
" intereft to be with me as much as
" poffible, in order to beat back *Cu-*
" *pid*, fhould he fee him making any
" advances towards me.——What fay
" you, my boy? Will you undertake
" to guard my heart from thofe pretty
" adventureffes who will, no doubt,
" try all their arts to entrap it ?"

" Though I could perceive joy
" dancing in the eyes of my *Edward*
" at this propofal, yet he modeftly
" declined giving his anfwer till I had
" declared my fentiments.

" Notwithstanding the thoughts
" of a feparation were almoft dreadful
" to me as death itfelf, yet could I
                              " object

" object to what appeared fo much
" for his advantage? How felfifh to
" have detained him!—Would his
" engaging company compenfate for
" thofe reflections I muft have felt
" from an ill-timed fondnefs, which
" had debarred him the opportunity
" of raifing a fortune adequate to his
" merit?

" REFLECTIONS fuch as thefe de-
" termined me, fuffer what I would,
" not to oppofe the generous intentions
" of my friend; and if I did not in
" reality confent with chearfulnefs,
" yet I tried at its appearance.

" THIS ready acquiefcence filled his
" honeft heart with rapture: he
" embraced firft me, then my fon,
" and declared a thoufand times it

" fhould

" should be his only study to make us
" happy.

" ALAS! my dear *Edward!* thy
" grateful acknowledgements to our
" benefactor, thy tender manly for-
" row at leaving me, I never, never
" shall forget.

" BEFORE their departure my friend
" put a paper into the hands of my
" son, desiring it might not be opened
" in his presence. When he left us,
" how were we overwhelmed by fresh
" acts of generosity! Enclosed were
" two letters; one to *Edward,* begging
" his acceptance of three hundred
" pounds, as I might be unadvised
" of (he said) the numberless things
" necessary for so long a voyage.

" THAT

" " THAT directed to me appeared a
" large packet, which on opening I
" found contained a fheet of parch-
" ment, together with the following
" note :

" OFTEN have you told me you
" wanted fome way in which to oblige
" me : I have now thought of a me-
" thod.—If you accept the enclofed,
" you lay me under infinite obliga-
" tions :—on the contrary, fhould you
" return it, I fhall for the future
" look on you as a perfon who refufes
" to gratify the warmeft wifh of my
" heart.—I intend fleeping with you
" to-night, when you will fix by your
" determination in this affair either
" the friendfhip or difapprobation of

" Your now affectionate, &c."

C 5 " On

" OH my dear Ladies! what think
" you it was he forced fo ftrenuoufly
" on my acceptance? No lefs than an
" annuity of two hundred pounds.—
" The pain I felt at being loaded with
" fuch immenfe favours, was fome-
" what leffened by the pleafure it gave
" my *Edward* to think that I fhould
" not be left deftitute.

" To fhorten my narrative, I can
" only fay I accepted this new obliga-
" tion, which I found it impoffible
" to refufe, but at the expence of
" that friendfhip I fo highly eftimated;
" and parted from my deareft child
" and his kind protector with more re-
" folution than I ever believed myfelf
" mafter of.

" DURING two years, I conftantly
" heard from my fon, whofe letters
were

" were filled with prayers for my
" health, and in repeating acts of ten-
" derness from our beft friend.

" AH my children! I can proceed
" no farther! Take this (drawing a
" letter from his pocket): I received
" it the third year after he left *Eng-*
" *land.* Wo is me! I cannot read it!
" A parent's grief obftruds my fight;
" I will retire, and indulge the effu-
" fions of my forrow."

SEEING him quit the room with
precipitation, " My God! faid
" *Maria:* how I tremble for the fate
" of this deferving youth! How I pity
" his forlorn parent! Why did he con-
" fent to his leaving *England?* But let
" us examine the letter he has left.
" May there not be a gleam of hope
" that he is yet living?

C 6   " OH

"Oh no! (cried she, after they
"had eagerly thrown their eyes over
"its contents) oh no! there is not
"the leaft fhadow of hope! Every
"flattering idea of that nature here
"vanifhes! Cruel, unpitying Elements!
"Was it neceffary for you to com-
"bine in the ruin of this accomplifhed
"youth, and to render miferable a
"poor old man, who had before
"tafted too deeply of Misfortune's cup?
"By Water he already has loft a be-
"loved wife and child : could not the
"unrelenting Fire have fpared the
"only remaining prop of his declin-
"ing age?"

To account for this tender forrow, which fprung fpontaneous
from the tender heart of Mifs *Coventry*, I fhall here oblige my readers
with a fight of the dreadful letter

Mr.

Mr. *Gore* left for their perufal, which
it feems came from the friend who
had kindly, but very unfortunately,
carried his fon from *England*.

LETTER.

" AH my friend! what can I fay!
" how adminifter comfort, who am
" myfelf deftitute of comfort? But if
" my feelings are fo great, what muft
" be thofe of a fond unhappy parent!
" I now behold my folly in taking
" your treafure from you; I fee it too
" late! Guefs the horrid cataftrophe.—
" If you do not, I fear I can never pre-
" vail on my trembling pen to tell it
" you. Yet, my good old friend,
" you muft know it! there is a cruel
" neceffity that you fhould.—Let me
" then, as a punifhment, take on my-
" felf the melancholy tafk of relating
it;

" it; for had it not been for me, your
" beloved and deferving child might
" have been perhaps at this very mo-
" ment fitting by your fide.

     " I said I would recount;—but
" where am I to begin? Had I been
" to write to you a week fince, I
" could with juftnefs have told you,
" that your dear *Edward* and myfelf
" were as happy as it was poffible for
" two people to be, who were fo dif-
" tant from their friends and native
" land : But how, in that fhort fpace,
" nay, in three days, fadly reverfed!

     " Our dear boy, for I fondly ufed
" to call him mine, had made an en-
" gagement with fome young gentle-
" men to go by water, on a party of
" pleafure, about three leagues. They
" were to return the next day; but at
                         " twelve

" twelve that fame night I was almoft
" rendered fpeechlefs with grief, by a
" meffenger who ran to inform me,
" the veffel in which **my** *Edward*
" went had by fome accident taken
" fire, and that it was impoffible to
" fend them any affiftance, the wind
" blowing frefh from the fhore.

" As foon as this fhocking account
" reached me, I haftened to the place
" where I was told this dreadful con-
" flagration was yet to be feen.

" HERE I drop the curtain : Happy
" fhould I have been to fay one fingle
" life was faved; that life our *Ed-*
" *ward's*. But alas! they all fhared
" the fame fate ; every creature pe-
" rifhed.

" AND

" And now, my dear miferable
" friend, what can I add? You are
" not at this hour, after undergoing
" fuch various and fevere trials, to be
" told on whom you are to rely. Ad-
" vice of this kind would be imperti-
" nent, as well as unneceffary. I fhall
" only, therefore, recommend you to
" that Power who can, when he
" pleafes, turn all our forrows into
" joy. Farewell, my dear friend; the
" fhip by which I fend this is now un-
" der fail. May Heaven give you
" comfort!"

Lavinia and Mifs *Coventry* had
been weeping over this epiftle, when
Mr. *Gore* and his nephew re-entered together. *Maria* met them at the door.
The former held out his hand: " My
" dear child (faid he), your eyes, as
" well

" well as thofe of the tender-hearted
" Mifs *Gilford*, fhew how they have
" been employed. Can I forgive my-
" felf for diftreffing you as I have
" done ?"

MISS *Coventry* involuntarily preffed
the fhrivelled hand which contained
hers to her lips. " My deareft father
" (replied fhe), you muft allow me a
" few tears for the lofs of my amiable
" brother. How fevere have been
" your afflictions! Yet you are hap-
" pier ftill than thoufands : a con-
" fcience fuch as you are poffeffed
" of is a continual fource of fatis-
" faction."

" BUT methinks, Sir, (added Mifs
" *Gilford*, taking his other hand) it is
" wrong to exclude yourfelf fo en-
" tirely

" tirely from fociety. Sorrow finks
" deepeft in the mind when it is
" nurfed in folitude. Company might
" have chafed away many gloomy re-
" flections, whilft in this place they
" muft receive addition."

" I cannot (replied Mr. *Harry*
" *Gore)* avoid diffenting from the opi-
" nion of my *Lavinia* ; for after the
" fhock I received from her fuppofed
" falfhood, nothing was fo tedious as
" being obliged to pafs a day even
" with my moft intimate friends; and
" I can truly fay, if I ever tafted the
" leaft fatisfaction, it was in retire-
" ment."

" THIS you alledge, I fuppofe, Sir
" (faid Mifs *Coventry)*, that you may
" be fet down in the lift of conftant
" lovers;

" lovers ; but fhould that be the cafe,
" I fancy you would meet with few
" names before your own."

" How hardly you think of our
" fex, Madam (replied he). May not
" that ficklenefs, of which I confefs
" we give but too many inftances, be
" fometimes owing to your own in-
" conftancy ?".

" Upon my honour (returned fhe),
" I can only anfwer your queftion in
" the words of Mr. *Addifon*, " Much
" may be faid on both fides."

" Lord blefs me (cried *Lavinia*) ! it
" is almoft dark, and Mr. *Coventry*
" will be again concerned at our ftay.
" Pray drop your contention, good
" people ; and, as we walk to our
" car-

" carriage, let us jointly requeſt our
" revered guide to finiſh his recital."

THE good man promiſed to comply; and neither of the gentlemen
preſſing them to ſtay longer, on account of the reaſon given by Miſs *Gil-*
ford for their return to *Weatly*, they
proceeded through the wood by ſlow
ſteps, liſtening to Mr. *Gore*, who in
this manner concluded his hiſtory.

CHAP.

C H A P. XVII.

" AFTER the letter you have juft
" read, you will not be fur-
" prifed at the refolution I took to re-
" tire from a world where I had expe-
" rienced for many years nothing but
" misfortunes.

" The cave which I had formerly
" feen in this wood again prefented it-
" felf to my remembrance, and im-
" mediately I refolved to make it the
" place of my retreat, unknowing and
" unknown. I was obliged to ac-
" quaint two people of my defign:
" Thefe were the honeft couple you
" have feen at my little habitation.
" They

" They had lived with me for twenty
" years; and their love and fidelity
" cannot be better expreſſed than in
" the reſolution they took to accom-
" pany me hither.

" ONE thing perplexed me greatly:
" I wanted to be thought dead by the
" world, particularly by my friend,
" from whoſe bounty I enjoyed an in-
" come for which I had now no uſe,
" and which I knew it was impoſſible
" for me to decline, till he ſhould be
" aſſured of my death.

" How to aſſure him of it, and re-
" ſtore his generous favours, was my
" only care; and having well conſi-
" dered this matter, I diſpatched
" *Simon* with a note to each printer
" of the daily papers, to ſignify my
" death.

" AFTER

" After this neceſſary caution, my
" next ſtep was to get, by the aſſiſt-
" ance of my two faithful domeſticks,
" the few conveniences with which I
" am here ſurrounded. *Simon* went
" often abroad, and heard my fate la-
" mented every where; no one be-
" lieved me living, and my unkind
" brother outwardly mourned for me;
" whilſt my dear nephew, I was in-
" formed, ſuffered real ſorrow."

" Indeed, Sir, I did (interrupted
" that young gentleman), and never
" can I forgive myſelf—"

" Hold ! (cried his uncle) I know
" what you would ſay, my child:
" Was it your fault that I had not be-
" fore received the tender offices of
" your dutiful affectionate heart ? No:
" the commands of your father obliged
                                    " you

" you to reſtrain thoſe warm ſentiments
" of love you entertained for me; ſen-
" timents which thoſe of my own *Ed-*
" *ward* hardly exceeded."

" Oh how good, how very kind,
" are you, my dear Sir (returned he)!
" Had my mother lived—But you
" know I loſt her in what may be called
" my infant ſtate. Had ſhe lived, ho-
" nouring your virtues as I know ſhe
" honoured them, I might have ſooner
" been permitted to pay you that du-
" tiful attendance which your good-
" neſs, your piety, your fortitude de-
" manded."

" Enough, enough, my ſon (ſaid
" the good man). Say no more;
" you ſoften me too much! I ſhall not
" be able to proceed with the little
" which remains to be told. It is only
" this,

" this, Ladies: That as foon as my
" brother paid the debt of nature, I
" caufed my being alive, with the place
" of my concealment, to be revealed
" by *Simon* to my nephew, who flew
" immediately to my expecting arms.
" After the firft tumults of his tran-
" fport were fomewhat abated, he
" ufed every argument his tendernefs
" could fuggeft to make me quit my
" Cave, and to go back with him to
" the *Grove*, where he kindly faid
" I fhould be intire mafter.

" SEEING he could not prevail, he
" caufed that houfe to be built which
" you have juft quitted; and to quiet
" his fears for my health, I promifed
" to retire every night to this more
" wholefome dwelling. And now, my
" dear children, I have opened to you
" the whole fcene of my diftreffes, I

" intreat, on my blefling, you will not
" let them affect your minds with me-
" lancholy.—Happier days may yet
" await me! If I ever hear the hands
" of my *Harry* and his amiable
" *Lavinia* are united, I think I may
" promife you I fhall again tafte of
" joy."

I SHALL not repeat what farther
paffed on this occafion: delight, gratitude, and reverence, filled every
breaft. Their feparation was neceffary, but painful. Another vifit was promifed by the ladies.
Their fervants and carriage were
now in view: they parted at the verge
of the wood; the gentlemen returning to their cell, and the ladies to
their chariot.

LAVINIA

LAVINIA being fet down at the *Grange*, afked a fervant what company was in the houfe, hearing voices in the dining-parlour.

" SIR *William More*, Madam, (re-
" plied he) Mr. *Perigreen*, and Mr.
" *Jones*, dined with my mafter."

FLUTTERED at the very name of Sir *William*, fhe afked for Lady *Gilford*; and being told fhe was in her drefling-room, afcended the ftairs, ordering the fellow not to tell Sir *Francis* fhe was come back.

HER mother, with a countenance not the moft pleafing, afked *Lavinia* the reafon why fhe had not returned the laft night. " Mifs *Coventry*'s com-
" pany (faid her Ladyfhip) is doubtlefs
" very agreeable ; yet fhe ought not, I

think,

" think, *Levy*, to engrofs fo much of
" yours. Here has been Sir *William*
" *More* twice to fee you, and great-
" ly difappointed to find you not at
" home.

" I THOUGHT, my dear Madam,
" (replied Mifs *Gilford*) you would
" have fpared me from the pain of
" again declaring I had rather die than
" be the wife of that man. Reflect
" on his vile artifice."

" I DO reflect on that affair," cried
her Ladyfhip with a voice in which anger was predominate; " I reflect on it
" with fhame, that a daughter of mine
" fhould be capable of a contrivance fo
" low to bribe a fervant. What mean-
" nefs!—

" AND

" And can you really, can my mo-
" ther believe me a wretch even more
" despicable than Sir *William?* Can
" she suppose me guilty of so dishonour-
" able a subterfuge?"

" What reason have I to acquit
" you?—Did not *James* overhear you
" offer the girl a hundred pounds to
" fasten the lye upon us?—Have I not
" discharged the creature? Has not Sir
" *William More* by the most solemn
" assertions convinced me of his inno-
" cence?"

" So you are determined, Madam,
" to believe this vile agent, and his
" still viler employer, before a daugh-
" ter who has never forfeited her duty
" or her Word."

" Child,

" Child, child, (in a tone of in-
" creafing difpleafure) we know your
" unaccountable averfion to this
" match."

" Will nothing, Madam, convince
" you of my innocence ? But fuppofe,
" after all his folemn affertions, you
" fhould hear Sir *William* confefs the
" truth of *Sally*'s information ?"

" Was he to do that indeed, I fhould
" think of him as he deferves."

" It fhall be fo, faid *Lavinia*," for
a moment loft in thought.

" What ?" afked her mother.

" First promife me, Madam, that
" if he owns himfelf author of this black
" affair, you will never more com-
" mand

"mand me to receive his very hateful
"vifits."

" I MAY venture to make you
" fuch a promife, on the terms you
" mention."

" Two things more I muft requeft :
" one, that your Ladyfhip will not
" acquaint my brother with what has
" now paffed between us: the other,
" that you will engage Sir *William* for
" to-morrow afternoon, when I pro-
" mife to be prefent, and hope to fatisfy
" your Ladyfhip of my innocence and
" his bafenefs."

" I COMPLY with this too, *Levy* ; but
" in return expect, if the guilt, inftead
" of falling on him fhould reft on your-
" felf, I fhall no longer find you re-
" fractory."

D 4

SIR

Sir *Francis* coming into the room at this inftant, prevented an anfwer to her laft fentence, not at all un-feafonable for *Lavinia*.

The Baronet being half-feas-over, told his fifter he came with a petition from Sir *William*, who had feen her enter the houfe, that fhe would permit him to attend her in the breakfaft-parlour, where he waited for that favour.

" Waiting for me! (cried *Lavi-*
" *nia*, her eyes expreffing indigna-
" tion) the man is furely poffeffed! Did
" I ever yet confent to fee him, with-
" out it was by the abfolute commands
" of my mother? and then did he not
" know my reluctance to obey? How,
" after this, can he defire me to come
" to

" to him, as if I would oblige him vo-
" luntarily?"

" Your diſlike, *Levy*, (replied Sir
" *Francis*) does not appear abated to
" Sir *William*. I think (applying to
" his mother) we muſt e'en let her
" have her own way."

" Ah now, indeed, (ſaid the grate-
" ful *Lavinia*) you are my kind bro-
" ther!"

" I hope (returned he in a whiſper)
" you have not forgot my intereſt with
" Miſs *Coventry*; for ſhould ſhe be as
" cruel to me as you are to the gentle-
" man below, depend on it, things
" will not wear ſo pleaſing a face: for
" aſſure yourſelf, that you yet ſhall
" be Lady *More*, if your friend does
" not conſent to be Lady *Gilford*."

" The

THE claret, of which Sir *Francis* had taken a sufficient quantity, stripped off that disguise he had hitherto assumed, and his sister found with inexpressible concern that it was as easy for an *Ethiopian* to change his skin, or a Leper his spots, as for Sir *Francis* to change his nature.—However, having great dependence on the next afternoon, she resolved to keep secret *Maria*'s disapprobation of his addresses, and to repay art with art: therefore, instead of appearing in the least shocked, she replied with a smile, that if her marriage with Sir *William* depended on Miss *Coventry*, she was certain never to be honoured with the title of Lady *More*.

THOUGH a double *entendre*, he took the meaning of this ambiguous expression in the manner he wished it; which

which put him in such high good-humour, that he swore he would go that
instant to Sir *William*, to let him know
his visits would no longer be agreeable
to the family.

He was actually going on this er-
rand, when Lady *Gilford* called him
back, and desired nothing might be
done in this affair till the next afternoon; and requested her son to engage him to give them his company
at that time, for some particular reasons.

" But what, Madam, says *Lavi-*
" *nia?*"

" I have no objection, brother,
" provided it is his last visit."

Sir

SIR *Francis* with an oath confirmed it fhould, and left the room, going immediately to the breakfaft-parlour, where he found Sir *William*, who was informed he could not prevail on his fifter to come down that night.

THE Baronet politely termed her a d—n--d pretty prude; an appellation for which he made no fort of apology to her brother; nor, indeed, did he feem to expect any.—After telling his friend Lady *Gilford*'s defire of feeing him the next afternoon, they went back to their company, where the bottle foon made Sir *William* forget the unkindnefs of his miftrefs.

LAVINIA, when fhe left her mother's apartment and retired to her own, began and finifhed a long letter to Mr. *Harry Gore*, the contents of

which

which never came to my knowledge:
only this I can inform my readers,
that it was fent to the *Grove* by a perfon in whom fhe could confide, early
the next morning; and that the anfwer fhe received from her lover filled
her eyes with additional luftre.

I SHALL pafs over many hours to
haften that time forward, which
was to produce Sir *William* his laft
interview with Mifs *Gilford*, who
that afternoon fparkled in all the or-
nament of drefs.

SIR *Francis* flattering himfelf that
Lavinia had the preceding night given
him hopes Mifs *Coventry* was not a-
verfe to his addreffes, put on an air of
good-humour, and eyeing her with a
fmile, " Upon my foul, *Levy*, (faid
" he) I am not furprifed at Sir *William*'s
" paffion.

" paffion. Such a girl is worth fome
" pains, by G—. I did not think till
" now you was half fo handfome!
" Yet how cruel to put on all thefe
" killing charms, when you are re-
" folved not to heal the wound you
" have given !"

" I EXPECT other company than
" Sir *William* (replied *Lavinia*): I
" have fent to defire Mr. *Coventry*,
" *Maria*, and the good Doctor will
" drink tea with us.—Blefs me ! they
" are come ! I fee their fervant this
" moment entering the houfe."

SIR *Francis* flew to affift them from
their carriage; but returned inftantly
with a difappointed countenance.

" DEVILISH unlucky, Sifter ! they
" are prevented, it feems. *Dick* tells
" me

" me there are four gentlemen and
" two ladies juſt come from *London*.
" But here is a billet for you."

Mɪss *Gilford* took the note, broke
the ſeal, ran her eye over it, then gave
it to her brother, ſaying, " Only an
" apology : they are kept from us by
" the arrival of Lord and Lady *L——*,
" and ſome of their friends."

" Cᴜʀsᴇ their friends ! But what
" other gentlemen ? Three, it ſeems.
" Confound them !"

" I ʜᴇᴀʀᴅ but of one ; and that one
" a ward of his Lordſhip's.

" Yᴏᴜɴɢ, handſome, and rich, no
" doubt.   Hell catch him ! I ſhall
" ſtand a fine chance.   But tell me,
" *Levy*——"

HᴇÏ

He was going to proceed, when the appearance of Sir *William More* put a ftop to his queftion; which, as it concerned the hint fhe had given the laft evening, might have puzzled her to anfwer.

Notwithstanding *Lavinia* knew what mortifications were preparing for Sir *William,* his prefence difconcerted her to fuch a degree, that fhe could hardly arife at his entrance.

There is fomething in guilt which cannot be concealed. The fight of the perfon injured, like *Ithuriel's* fpear, brings it to light, though hidden in the bottom of the heart. The livid pale, the confcious blufh, the hefitating accent, are fo many witneffes to condemn the injurer.

Sir

SIR *William* was diftinguifhed by each of thofe. Though naturally a bold, a forward man, the fight of Mifs *Gilford* made him turn now pale, then red. He would have fpoke: " Ma-" dam (he did fay), to be fure you, " you, you have heard—" He ftopt here.

" Pox take it (cried Sir *Francis*)! " what a fool does this Love make " thee!"

" You miftake, brother (faid *Lavi-* " *nia*); Sir *William*'s confufion arifes " from another motive than Love. I " think, Sir (turning to him, with an " air of irony), this is the firft oppor-" tunity I have had to afk your pardon " for the vile means I made ufe of to " fully your unblemifhed charafter."

LADY

LADY *Gilford* coming in juft as this blow had almoft levelled Sir *William* even with defpair, her prefence re-affured him a little; and paying his refpects to her Ladyfhip, he had the courage to tell *Lavinia*, that, " By " Heaven, he was unconfcious of her " meaning."

" You are very good, Sir (replied " fhe, in her former tone), not to un- " derftand me. I am fenfible of your " generofity: You would not cover " me with confufion before my mo- " ther, before my brother, by up- " braiding me with the bribe I gave " my fervant to traduce you."

" By the great God, Madam (rifing " in a paffion), I never faid you had " bribed the wench; I only declared " my

" my own innocence; and here again
" I proteft by all—"

" STOP, Sir (interrupted Mifs *Gil-*
" *ford,* with a fweet dignity); utter
" not the horrid perjury, at leaft till
" I bring one witnefs to prove your
" guilt."

MISS *Gilford* receiving no reproof
for this fpirited behaviour, made Sir
William fee how matters ftood; for
which reafon he determined to throw
up the game; and what made him
more fixed on this ftep was the lady's
hint of a witnefs. *James,* for inte-
refted confiderations, would not, he
very well knew, betray him.

WHO, then, could be this dreaded
evidence? Not Mr. *Gore*; no, it could
not be him, after the convincing proofs
he

he fuppofed fhe had given of her love for another. Yet, on a fecond confideration, it was not impoffible. There was even a probability that they might by fome accident have come to an eclairciffement. A very thought of this nature worked fo powerfully on his coward imagination, that he fancied he faw Mr. *Gore* at that inftant with his fword drawn, breathing defiance and revenge; a fuggeftion which drove the daftard blood from his before crimfoned cheeks.

HAVING nothing to fay in his defence, he fcowled a look of difdain from under his bent brows; replying, with a tremendous oath, " Such ufage was not to be borne; and never more would he trouble himfelf about a proud imperious woman."

THIS

THIS he faid whilft he held the door in his hand.

LADY *Gilford* rifing, darted a look of difpleafure at her daughter, and was advancing to detain Sir *William*, when that gentleman's ears were faluted by a voice which threw him into an univerfal tremor. Though, to the delighted ones of *Lavinia*, harmony itfelf, the trembling Baronet miftook its mufic for the hoarfe notes of a raven croaking out his final diffolution.

MR. *Gore*, for it was no other, flafhing upon them with the dignity of confcious virtue, prevented his coward rival from paffing the door ; and faid, forcing him back,

" EXCUSE

"EXCUSE me, Sir, if I compel you
"to return. Sir *Francis*, Lady *Gil-*
"*ford*, and her charming daughter,
"if I was not to acknowledge the
"large debt I owe you, would un-
"doubtedly defpife me, as a man
"without gratitude. May I hope
"your Ladyfhip, and you, Sir (grace-
"fully turning to Sir *Francis*), will
"pardon the liberty I am about to
"take, by afking this gentleman a few
"queftions in your prefence?"

THEY only bowed their heads:
They knew not what to anfwer, fo
much were they aftonifhed at the appearance of Mr. *Gore*, but more by
the manner in which he accofted Sir
William, and the vifible guilt of that
unworthy incendiary.

LAVINIA

LAVINIA, by whom this laſt viſitor was not unexpected, having ſent that morning to contrive an interview from which ſhe flattered herſelf with the moſt pleaſing conſequences, gave her lover, when ſhe ſaw him force back Sir *William*, a look which ſpoke even more plain than words, and told him he ſhould not carry matters too far; which reminded him of the promiſe he had made his uncle the preceding day; which intreated him, if he loved her, not to hazard his valuable life againſt the moſt deſpicable of God's creatures.

IN the ſame ſilent language he bad her not to be alarmed: he aſſured her, the known cowardice of his adverſary would prevent every thing ſhe feared.

" Now,

" Now, Sir," cried Mr. *Gore*, indignation darting from his determined
eye, whilſt the delinquent vile ſeemed
to ſhrink into himſelf, " Now, Sir, I
" am at your ſervice. Though there
" are, I know, to a generous perſon
" few ſubjeċts more ungrateful than to
" hear thoſe praiſes they deſerve, yet
" with or without your leave, Sir *Wil-*
" *liam*, I will, I muſt mention ſome
" of the many favours you have be-
" ſtowed on me ; ſo many, I muſt
" thank you for them too."

" Sɪʀ—Sir—I don't know—I don't
" underſtand———"

" You have convinced me that you
" neither know or underſtand the laws
" of honour, conſcience, humanity.
" What I now declare (continued Mr.
" *Gore*, applying himſelf to Lady *Gil-*
" *ford*

" *ford* and Sir *Francis*) may appear ex-
" tremely unpolite; but politeneſs has
" no part to take in this affair. Your
" daughter, Madam, your ſiſter, Sir,
" has been traduced, vilely traduced
" by this wretch, I will not call him
" man: he ſhall himſelf prove to you
" he deſerves the appellation.

" TAKE care, Sir, (ſaid Sir *Francis*
" in an angry tone) take care! I will
" not ſuffer this in my houſe: Sir
" *William More* ſhall not be thus
" treated."

" PARDON me, Sir *Francis*, I came
" not here to have any altercation with
" the brother of Miſs *Gilford*."

" PRAY, Brother, pray, Madam,
" (for Lady *Gilford* was going to ſay
" ſomething) in defence of my ho-
VOL. I.   E   " nour,

" nour, in defence of the honour of my
" family, of my fex, permit Mr.
" *Gore* to proceed.—This man (look-
" ing difdainfully on Sir *William*)
" has been too much liftened to al-
" ready."

" I THINK we muft comply (faid
" her Ladyfhip), indeed, if Sir *Wil-*
" *liam* has————"

" PARDON me, Madam (inter-
" rupted Mr. *Gore*); if I do not con-
" vince you he has been the moft de-
" figning, the blackeft of villains, ba-
" nifh me your prefence; call me, if
" poffible, a bafer, a more fubtle
" villain than I now call Sir *Wil-*
" *liam.*"

NOTHING but fear of offending his
fifter, and deftroying his intereft with
Mifs

Miſs *Coventry*, could have reſtrained
the fury of Sir *Francis*; whilſt his
friend turned a deaf ear to Mr. *Gore*'s
laſt threats, talking loudly and ear-
neſtly to Sir *Francis*, and attempting
to defend himſelf; though, in fact,
he was thrown into ſo terrible a fright,
that he hardly knew what he ſaid or
did.

MR. *Gore* advancing towards him
with a threatening countenance, his
hand upon his ſword, " Anſwer me,
" Sir *William* (cried he), the queſtions
" I propoſe;—anſwer them without
" evaſion.

" DID you tell me Miſs *Gilford*
" every evening entertained a fa-
" voured lover? Did you carry me to
" the window, where you aſſured
" me they met? Did you there ſub-

E 2   " ſtitute

" ftitute *Sally* to perfonate her Lady?
" Was I deceived by your arts to be-
" lieve, againft the evidence of my
" heart, to believe I faw Mifs *Gilford*
" at the window entertaining a lover
" unworthy of herfelf and family?—
" Give me a true, give me an
" immediate anfwer, or, coward
" as thou art, thy life fhall be the
" forfeit."

SIR *William*, who already fancied he faw the fword of his determined adverfary drawn from its
fcabbard, looked now on this fide—
then on that—went to the window—
threw it up—let it down again ;—and
though half dead with fear, attempted
at a carelefs unconcerned air.

SEEING his irrefolution, Mr. *Gore*
again demanded an anfwer, or, if he

longer

longer refufed to give it, in the
moft determined manner infifted on
his going with him to a proper
place, where he would force it
from him by another method than
words.

SIR *William*, finding he had but
one alternative, either to fight or own
himfelf a rafcal, did not long hefitate
which to chufe : The former it could
not be ; his heart affirmed it ; confol-
ing himfelf, if he preferred the latter,
his title and fortune would ftill command refpect from a great part of man-
kind.

BEING once come to a final refolution, firft getting as near the door
as poffible, he delivered the following
eloquent harangue :

" DEVIL

"Devil fetch me, Mr. *Gore,* if
" you are not a curfed unaccount-
" able perfon! I am not afraid, d'ye
" fee; no, damme if I am! So far
" from repenting what I have done,
" I fhall glory in telling you, that I
" did contrive a curfed clever revenge.
" Confound my ftars, that it has not
" been more fuccefsful!" Saying which,
and the lock anfwering to his extended
hand, he made but one ftep to the fervants hall, ordered the coachman to get
immediately on his box, bouncing into his chariot, which carried or rather flew with him out of the court-
yard. But it is no more our intention
to purfue him, than it was Mr. *Gore's*:
for this reafon we return to the draw-
ing-room, where we fhall find the
hero who had drove not the lion, but
a much lower animal, happy beyond
his moft fanguine expectations.

LADY

LADY *Gilford* and Sir *Francis* had
already thanked him for bringing to
light the hidden villainy of Sir *William*.
" The vile man! How could they
" ever have fuppofed him guilty of
" fuch an action !" *Lavinia* was com-
manded by her mother, defired by
her brother, to be grateful to Mr.
Gore.

WHAT, at that moment, was the
joy of both! It cannot be defcribed!
It muft be left to the imagination of
my readers.

SIR *Francis*, after tea, faying he
had an engagement with Mr. *Jones*,
took his leave ; and a fervant entering
foon after, and delivering her Ladyfhip a letter, fhe likewife retired to
read it.

THE lovers being left alone, expreffed the almoft inexpreffible pleafure they felt at the charming profpects
before them.

" NOTHING now, my deareft *La-*
" *vinia,* (faid Mr. *Gore*) will ob-
" ftruct our happinefs. Your mother,
" nay even your brother feems to fa-
" vour my pretenfions: I am full of
" the moft pleafing hopes."

" NEITHER am I lefs happy, but
" rather lefs fanguine (replied Mifs
" *Gilford* fmiling). My brother at
" prefent is, indeed, very kind; but
" he has finifter views in this kindnefs.
" In them he muft be difappointed;
" and if he fhould again become our
" enemy, we have nothing to hope
" from the favour of my mother."

JUST

Just as she had pronounced these words, Lady *Gilford* with a countenance of some concern and great business rushed into the room: " Child
" (said her Ladyship), we must set
" out this instant for your aunt *Grosvenor*'s.

" I hope, Madam, my dear aunt
" is not ill."

" Very ill, indeed! Poor, dear,
" good woman! her physician has
" pronounced she cannot live eight
" hours."

" Bless me! how I am terrified!
" Who brought your Ladyship this
" intelligence?" said *Lavinia*.

" The letter I just now received:
" it came by an express.—*Stephens*

E 5 " wrote

" wrote it.—She fays her Lady is
" very ill, very ill, indeed.—Alas!
" my poor dear fifter! fhe has a large
" fortune to bequeath.—Lord help
" me! how unlucky Sir *Francis* is not
" in the houfe! I have fent a meffen-
" ger.—I hope he is not gone far; I
" hope he will be met with at Mr.
" *Jones's.*—A fad ftroke, Mr. *Gore!*
" Juft turned of fifty!—My fifter is
" no more!"

HERE the meffenger fhe had difpatched for Sir *Francis* returned to
tell her Ladyfhip, he could not be
found.

" WELL, (cried fhe) it is very un-
" fortunate; but we muft go without
" him; there is no time to be loft:
" it is forty miles to *Millbridge.* Is
                                        " the

" the coach ready? Order it to the
" door inftantly."

THE fervant bowed, and difappeared.

MR. *Gore* defired the honour to ef-
cort them ; which being granted, after handing the Ladies to their carriage, he ftepped in himfelf, and,
feated oppofite to his *Lavinia*, the
fix hours they were on the road feemed
but as one moment.

HER Ladyfhip being thoughtful,
he had an opportunity of entertaining his fair miftrefs without re-
ftraint.

ON their arrival at *Millbridge*, they
were met by Mrs. *Stephens*, who told

E 6   Lady

Lady *Gilford* with an air of real joy, that her fifter was out of danger.

I would not be thought to infinuate that her Ladyfhip was difpleafed at this intelligence; yet certain it is, fhe afked with a kind of fretful peevifhnefs, if that was the cafe, why was fhe wrote to in fuch a violent hurry, and obliged to fet out at an hour fo unfeafonable?

Mrs. *Stephens*, by way of an excufe, alledged her Lady's diforder had been a fudden fwelling in her throat; that at the time the meffenger was difpatched, fhe lay fpeechlefs; and it was then the opinion of doctor *Watkins* fhe could not out-live the night: but, contrary to the expectations of all about her, the fwelling broke three hours before her Ladyfhip's arrival,

fince

since which she had been and still continued in a sweet sleep.

LAVINIA felt sincere satisfaction on hearing this account. Mrs. *Grosvenor* was a most deserving woman, and had ever shewn the fondest affection for her niece. With pleasure would Miss *Gilford* have dedicated great part of her time to this amiable relation; but her mother had never cordially relished her since the death of Mr. *Grosvenor*, for doing an act of exalted generosity, which, for example sake, I shall here give my readers.

A NIECE of Mr. *Grosvenor*'s, a good and amiable girl, had engaged her affections to a worthy young man. This uncle, on whom was her sole dependance, obstinately opposed their union. His notions of ancestry were strained; he
thought

thought Mr. *Difney* undeferving his al-
liance, becaufe he could not trace
back his family more than a hundred
years.

EVERY argument was ufed to make
him recede from a refolution never to
give Mifs *Flewin* fixpence if fhe married Mr. *Difney*; but they were ufed
without fuccefs; he carried his obfti-
nacy to the grave.

AFTER his deceafe, on examining
the will, it appeared he had be-
queathed five thoufand pounds to his
niece, provided fhe gave her hand to
Sir *Toby Cummings*, a man of great family, without one other fingle recom-
mendation; but in cafe fhe refufed to
marry Sir *Toby*, that fum, together with
all the reft of his fortune, devolved to
his widow.

MISS

MISS *Flewin* did not repine at this hard fentence. Her tears fhe would have fuppreffed ; but as that was im-poffible, fhe took an opportunity to leave the room.

MRS. *Grofvenor* obferved her diftrefs, and followed the almoft heart-broken girl. " I am come, my dear Mifs " *Flewin* (faid fhe, taking her hand), " to do all in my power to wipe away " thefe tears. Every body, my love, " has failings ; your deferving uncle " was not exempt from them. But " let us remember only his virtues; to " do which, you muft oblige me by " accepting your legacy, without con- " ditions;" faying which fhe turned from her, not waiting a reply.

THIS action of Mrs. *Grofvenor* had in it fomething fo heinous in the eyes

of

of Lady *Gilford*, that, inſtead of giving thoſe praiſes certainly her due, ſhe
left the houſe in a pet, ſaying, " Since
" her thouſands were ſo plenty, her
" own nephew and niece might, ſhe
" thought, have come in for a ſhare :".
And probably but for this illneſs a re-
conciliation might never have been ef-
fected ; Mrs. *Groſvenor* reſenting her
ſiſter's behaviour; rightly judging ſhe
was at liberty to do as ſhe pleaſed with
her own fortune.

BUT to return to Lady *Gilford*, *La-*
vinia, and Mr. *Gore*, who we left in
a parlour below, the two former waiting till Mrs. *Groſvenor* ſhould awake,
to go to her ; an event that happened
juſt as they had refreſhed themſelves
with a diſh of tea.

THE

THE meeting between the two fifters was moft affecting on the part of Mrs. *Grofvenor*. She really loved Lady *Gilford*, though fhe defpifed her narrow way of thinking and acting. As for *Lavinia*, fhe beftowed on her the fondeft careffes, which were returned with affectionate engaging tendernefs.

A WEEK's confinement fo far completed the recovery of this good lady, that fhe left her room at the end of that time, impatient to pay her refpects to one of her vifitors, whom fhe had not yet feen, *Lavinia* having greatly prepoffeffed her in favour of Mr. *Gore* ; and no fooner did fhe fee him than he eftablifhed himfelf in her good opinion. She determined from this moment not to let fo charming a pair leave her houfe till fhe had feen

their

their nuptials folemnized; knowing the character of her nephew, and the treatment his fifter had met from him. Not that *Lavinia* had mentioned a fyllable to her of his unkindnefs: No, fhe was too generous even to wifh he might be leffened in the efteem of a perfon from whom he had expectations. Yet her aunt had heard it from others: Common **Fame** is no keeper of fecrets.

HAVING been at *Millbridge* three weeks, and the young folks one morning walked out together, Mrs. *Grofvenor* took the opportunity of being alone with Lady *Gilford*, to defire her Ladyfhip would the next morning beftow a very deferving girl on a worthy lover, who was prepared to receive her as the beft gift of Heaven. "I " had fome thoughts (continued fhe) " to

" to have given her away myself; but,
" for particular reasons, Sister, I now
" desire that favour of you."

" WITH all my heart (replied
" she); but as I am unacquainted
" with the lady, or her intended huf-
" band, and the marriage fo near,
" will it not appear odd for a ftran-
" ger—"

" NOT in the leaft (interrupted
" Mrs. *Grofvenor*). I will take on
" myfelf to anfwer for the propriety of
" your doing this kind office; and alfo
" that my friends will be very happy
" in your affiftance."

" WELL, but, Sifter (faid Lady *Gil-*
" *ford*), I wifh you could procure me
" an interview with them before to-
" morrow,

" morrow, or I fhall look mightily
" aukward."

" NOTHING can be more fortunate
" (replied fhe): They drink tea with
" me this afternoon. But, as other
" company may happen in at the
" fame time, before fhe enters the
" room I will place this ring on her
" finger, by which you may diftin-
" guifh her."

" GIVE me leave to look at it (faid
" Lady *Gilford*). It is an immenfe
" fine brilliant!—Well, I proteft!—
" Worth at leaft five hundred pounds!
" But you are ufed to make princely
" prefents, Sifter." This fhe faid, accompanied by a violent tofs of the
head; the five thoufand pounds beftowed on Mrs. *Difney* coming at that
inftant frefh to her memory.

" I AL-

"I ALWAYS (returned Mrs. *Grofve-*
"*nor*) confult the happinefs of thofe
"I love. Heaven, Lady *Gilford*, has
"bleffed me with riches. Can I,
"then, put them to a better ufe than
"by fecuring felicity to others? I feel
"a pleafure arifing from it not in the
"power of hoarded millions to be-
"ftow. Befides, the lady this ring is
"defigned for you will, after you are
"acquainted with her, love equal to
"myfelf."

"NOT I, indeed (returned her La-
"dyfhip, with a fneer). The perfon
"you appear fo amazingly fond of,
"may, for aught I know, be deferv-
"ing; but, upon my word, I have
"no notion of your violent regards.
"I have children to enjoy my for-
"tune. But if Heaven had not
"bleffed me with them, I fhould al-
"ways

" ways have confidered relations be-
" fore ftrangers."

THOUGH this hint was pretty plain,
Mrs. *Grofvenor* made no anfwer, but
broke off the converfation by afking
her ladyfhip to take a walk in the
fhrubbery. " The weather is fo fine
" (faid fhe), that it is really a fin to
" fit within doors. Mr. *Gore* and my
" niece are of the fame opinion. I
" fancy we fhall find them in the elm
" walk."

SHE was right in this conjecture:
Lavinia and her happy lover were
placed beneath one of the loftieft
trees, on an elegant Chinefe feat, and
fo much engaged by a *tête-à-tête*, of
what nature my readers are left to
imagine, that they did not perceive
the

the approach of the two ladies, till they came clofe upon them.

" KEEP your feat, my dears (faid
" Mrs. *Grofvenor*) ; if we difturb you,
" we are gone this moment."

" YOUR prefence muft always give
" me pleafure, Madam (replied *La-*
" *vinia*)."

" YOU are a little infinuater, my
" dear child. But come, Sifter, pray
" be feated. *Lavinia*, fit by me.
" Mr. *Gore* and your mamma fhall
" marfhal themfelves as they pleafe."

MR. *Gore* took his place on the other fide of Mifs *Gilford* ; his manly face, if I may be permitted the expreffion, gracefully confufed ; which
received

received no fmall addition from the
blufhing cheeks of his miftrefs.

"I wanted to fee, I wanted to
"talk to you (continued Mrs. Grofve-
"nor). I have been faying to my
"fifter, that to-morrow we are to have
"a wedding in our village: her Lady-
"fhip has promifed to give away the
"bride. Now tell me, Lavinia, tell
"me, Mr. Gore, will you grace our
"feftival with your prefence?"

"Dear, dear Madam (faid her
"trembling niece), can I refufe Mr. —
"Blefs me, what a fool! you, I meant,
"any thing in my power? But what
"fays my mother?

"I have no objection (returned her
"Ladyfhip), fince your aunt defires it."
"As

" For me, Madam, you know my
" heart (faid Mr. *Gore*); words there-
" fore are unneceffary." .

" Thank you, thank you (cried
" fhe, fmiling on each, and taking the
" hand of her niece). The bride, my
" dear, is thought to have one of the
" fineft hands in the world; let me
" fee if a bauble will add any thing to
" its beauty." At the fame time taking the brilliant from her finger, fhe put
it on *Lavinia's*.

At this moment Mr. *Gore* threw
himfelf at the feet of Lady *Gilford*,
entreating fhe would confirm the delightful hope Mrs. *Grofvenor's* words
had made him entertain.

" Indeed, Sifter (faid that gene-
" rous woman, I fhall be unhappy

" unlefs

" unlefs you pardon the little arti-
" fice I have ufed; and convince
" me of it, by confenting to join
" the hands of *Lavinia* and her lo-
" ver, who are only worthy of each
" other."

" You have greatly furprized me
" (replied her Ladyfhip)! So foon as
" to-morrow! Impoffible! It cannot
" be! Rife, Mr. *Gore* (in a voice not
" the moft harmonious); *Lavinia* and
" you are both to blame."

" NOT in the leaft (faid her fifter).
" If there is any blame, let it fall on
" me. The contrivance was all my
" own; nor do I think it a bad one.
" What objection can you have? I fup-
" pofe you fome day or other intend
" they fhall marry."

" I DO

" I do (she replied); but I can
" start ten thousand objections why it
" cannot be so soon as to-morrow."

" Give us ten, out of that multi-
" plicity," said Mrs. *Grosvenor* smiling.

" Well, then, to satisfy you in
" the first place, my son will know
" nothing of the matter; and un-
" doubtedly must take it very ill, that
" I have disposed of his sister without
" consulting him."

" Psha! leave that affair to me;
" and if I do not satisfy him, why—I
" will do all I can to unmarry them
" again."

" I cannot bear this, Sister; it is
" treating me so much like a child."

F 2

" Right;

" Right ; and I look on your ob-
" jection as a very childifh one."

" What! I fuppofe too you would
" have my daughter marry without a
" fettlement ? "

" Not fo, neither, my good Sifter.
" I mind the main chance, though not
" perhaps quite fo much as yourfelf.
" But, to fhew you I have not neg-
" lected it in regard to my niece, —for
" the laft four days two lawyers of
" eminence have been bufily employed
" in forwarding the writings. Mr.
" *Gore*, on *Wednefday* laft, difpatched
" a meffenger to his fteward for the
" rent-roll of his eftate, ordering thofe
" gentlemen to fettle it entirely on
" your daughter. As to my niece's
" fortune, I have taken the liberty to
" add

" add ten thoufand pounds to the five
" thoufand left her by her father. Now
" if you forgive me, join the hands of
" this amiable pair."

Mr. *Gore* and *Lavinia*, at the beginning of this converfation, receiving
a filent hint from Mrs. *Grofvenor*, retired at a diftance.

" There is no refifting fo much
" generofity (replied Lady *Gilford*).
" Lead me, my dear Sifter, to this de-
" ferving man.   What! fettle his
" whole eftate on *Lavinia!* And you,
" too, give her ten thoufand pounds!
" How can we ever return fuch obli-
" gations?"

" You more than repay them in
" granting my requeft," faid Mrs.

Grofvenor;

Grofvenor; and taking her hand, led her to the Orangery, where a few minutes before fhe had feen the lovers enter.

I AM not going to defcribe their meeting. All was joy and tranfport, no doubt, on the part of Mr. *Gore*. As for *Lavinia*, modefty, gratitude, and love, had poffeffion of every feature.

MRS. *Grofvenor*, by an agreeable vivacity, prevented her niece from thinking too ferioufly on an approaching event. The fpirits of Lady *Gilford* had never before been fo truly harmonized: She faid a thoufand obliging things, both to her daughter and Mr. *Gore*. She even forgot Sir *Francis*; or elfe, if thought of in this

agreeable

agreeable hurry of affairs, it was not with her usual fear of offending him.

HERE wishing my readers a *bon repos,* I take my leave for the night, thinking so important an event as the wedding of Miss *Gilford,* deserves a new chapter.

F 4   CHAP.

✳✳✳✳✳✳✳✳✳✳✳✳✳✳✳✳

C H A P. XVIII.

" THE dawn is overcaſt, the morning lours," ſays the ſon of *Cato*.
But this was not the caſe at *Millbridge*; for I have been told from
good authority, that the ſun never
ſhone more dazzlingly bright than on
the morning when Miſs *Gilford* became Mrs. *Gore* ; perhaps with an intention to outvie the beauteous bluſh-
ing bride.

As this marriage will be kept a ſe-
cret ſome days, till *Lavinia* gets her
cloaths from *London*, I ſhall leave her
at *Millbridge*, and ſtep back to Miſs
Coventry.——Alas, my gentle reader,
how

how am I fhocked, how furprized, to find the alteration which has happened in that young lady in the three weeks we have been from *Weatly*? Where are her rofy cheek, fparkling eyes, and ruby lips? Where are they all fled? Some reafon there muft be for this fudden change! She affures her anxious father fhe was never better; to Lord, to Lady *L*—— fhe fays the fame; nor will fhe own her malady even to her favourite Dr. *Edgcombe*. If her diforder is not a bodily one, it is proper her mind fhould undergo an examination: For fhould it be feated there, the longer it continues undifco-vered, the more difficult to eradicate. It cannot be the abfence of her fair friend fhe regrets: She is not of a felfifh difpofition: *Maria* rejoices in the happinefs of Mrs. *Gore*, and has written her a letter of congratulation.

F 5   Does

Does she dislike her noble relations ? Her conduct affirms the contrary: She watches their looks for opportunities to oblige; whilst they appear to doat on their charming cousin.

She admires Miss *Hastings*; nor is she less pleased with Mr. *Stormont*, who are tenderly attached to each other.

Mr. *Vaughan* and his son come the last under my observation. The former of these, a very facetious old gentleman, is also in high favour with Miss *Coventry*. But as to the latter, I know not what to say: Her behaviour to him has something in it of restraint, yet blended with no tincture of dislike. Indeed, it would be unaccountable if it had ; Mr. *Edward Vaughan* being the object of general admiration.

Some

Some admired the charms of his perfon ; others his fenfe, his affability, his
noble air, his winning fweetnefs, the
harmony of his voice : The good revere him for his virtues ; their oppo-
fites for telling them their faults, if
under the difagreeable neceffity of doing it, in fo mild, fo friendly a manner,
as divefted reproof of its keen edge.

A LITTLE elf is juft perched on
my pen, and, in compaffion to my ftu-
pidity, makes a difcovery, which, perhaps, without his affiftance, I fhould
not have been able to make. Many
of my readers, I dare fay, who have
more experience in thefe matters,
might have found out that Mr. *Edward Vaughan*, though not from any
diflike, was the fole caufe of that alteration fo vifible in the lovely face of
Maria.

How

How does the fly urchin delight to hoodwink thofe he has rendered obedient to his power? Mifs *Coventry* really thought for many days, that thofe praifes fhe gave the graceful youth, whenever he was abfent, were only an echo to thofe fhe heard from every other mouth. She did not know, or at leaft would not allow herfelf to believe, her heart was any ways concerned in them. It was but four days fince, as I could find by my little affiftant, that fhe had made the important difcovery of its real fituation. To that moment, or rather fome time before, I fhall go back for the intelligence of my readers.

MISS *Coventry* had always thought her heart invulnerable. She had, hitherto, indeed, felt the moft perfect indifference. Love had ever been a
ftranger

ftranger to her bofom. Her father,
the good Doctor, and *Lavinia*, had till
now poffeffed it entirely. Mr. *Vaughan*
and his fon were but juft come from
abroad; the elder gentleman an intimate friend of Lord *L——*, and at his
requeft accompanied the party we
have already mentioned to *Hartly-
Row*. After his Lordfhip had embraced
Mifs *Coventry*, and introduced to her
his Lady and Mifs *Haflings*, he next
prefented both Mr. *Vaughans*, as friends
he very warmly efteemed.

MARIA received them with fuch
inimitable eafe, fuch true politenefs,
with looks fo fweetly modeft, with
fmiles fo irrefiftibly pleafing, that poor
Edward gazed firft, then liftened, and
paid his heart a forfeit to the interview.

NEVER

NEVER was a paffion more fudden or more violent than his. It could be exceeded by nothing but his refpect for the perfon who created it. True love is ever diffident. He feared by a difcovery of his, to offend the woman on earth he moft wifhed to oblige. But as a fire fmothered will fometimes flame, fo that lighted in the bofom of Mr. *Edward Vaughan*, notwithftanding all his endeavours to conceal it, foon blazed out, and became revealed to *Maria*.

ONE day, the weather being remarkably fine, Mr. *Coventry* propofed bowling. His daughter begged to be excufed, as fhe wanted to finifh a letter to Mrs. *Gore*; but the company with difficulty accepting her excufe, fhe promifed to join them on the Green,

after

after having difpatched fome family-
affairs which required her prefence.

Just as fhe had fettled her little
matters with the houfekeeper, and was
preparing to follow her friends, *Edward*, who had thought the time of
feparation long, came in purfuit of
her.

" I am an intruder, my dear Mifs
" *Coventry* (faid he, taking her hand
" refpectfully) ; yet I come, Madam,
" from the company, impatient that
" you deprive them fuch an age of
" your agreeable prefence."

" Why ftyle yourfelf an intruder
" (replied *Maria*, fmiling), when you
" bring fo flattering a meffage ? Is it
" poffible my friends, who are fo pleaf-
                              " ingly

" ingly amufed, could beftow a
" thought on me?"

" IT is plain Mifs *Coventry* is in-
" fenfible to her own value, or fhe
" would elfe know it was not in the
" power of any amufement to com-
" penfate for her abfence.

" POLITENESS in you, Sir, is habi-
" tual; but pray forbear to lavifh it
" on us poor country girls. If you
" fhould talk in this ftrain, we pof-
" fibly may not underftand it. Our
" rural fwains are all ruftic fimpli-
" city."

" I ENVY, Madam, thofe fwains
" (fighing). How ferene, how calm
" do they pafs through life!"

" PERHAPS.

" PERHAPS not so serenely as you
" suppose : They have troubles, I
" dare say, with which we are unac-
" quainted. But what think you, Mr.
" *Vaughan* (continued she, laughing),
" of a trial to convince you of your
" error ? Are you willing to exchange
" your laced coat for a russet frock ?
" Your hair you may still keep ; only
" it must be cropped close, and
" combed sleek on your forehead.
" And now what say you to my
" scheme ?"

" THAT I embrace it with rapture,
" on condition you permit me to
" chuse my shepherdess. Grant me
" but that, and you shall see the me-
" tamorphose in an instant."

" WHAT you ask (said *Maria*,
" visibly confused) is not in my power
" to

" to grant: But this I promife, when
" you reveal the name of your fa-
" vourite nymph, if I fhould happen
" to be acquainted with her, I will ufe
" my intereft in your favour."

" I REQUEST no more (he replied,
" kiffing her not-withdrawn hand).
" Whifper to your gentle bofom, that
" I can never love any but the divine
" Mifs *Coventry*."

MARIA's blufhing cheek, her whole
fweetly-abafhed face, might, had he
been lefs diffident, have given him
hopes that the declaration of his paffion had not offended: But as lovers
conftrue every thing wrong, he imagined he faw anger and refentment
arife in that breaft where it had never
yet entered.

" MY

" My dear Miss *Coventry* (conti-
" nued he), pardon my prefumption.
" My offence was unpremeditated.　I
" would have kept the fecret of my
" heart; but it efcaped me inadver-
" tently.　Do not, moft lovely of
" women, kill me with this cruel
" filence.　Speak to me; tell me only
" that I have not offended paft for-
" givenefs."

" WHAT would you have me fay,
" Mr. *Vaughan*," afked the trembling
Maria?

" SAY, my heavenly creature, I am
" not your averfion."

" MY averfion (repeated fhe, fweetly
" blufhing)! Does not my father,
" does not the good Doctor, do not
" Lord and Lady *L*—, all highly re-
" gard

" gard you ? How then can you be
" my averfion ? "

" ANGELIC goodnefs (he replied) !
" But you know not, Madam, to what
" a height I would afpire. Your
" heart is the ineftimable prize I feek,
" and muft be miferable if you refufe
" it. Confider—"

" I CONSIDER nothing (interrupted
" fhe, with a fmile which diffufed in-
" expreffible pleafure to the foul of
" Mr. *Vaughan*) but that you are an
" encroacher, and that I have liftened
" too long. A pretty *tête-à-tête* truly !
" What, I fuppofe you really think
" you fee before you a *Daphne* or a
" *Sylvia*, and, in return, I am to ima-
" gine you transformed to a faithful
" *Coridon*."

THE

THE entrance of the elder Mr.
Vaughan prevented a reply.

" JUST as I expected, juſt as I ex-
" pected (holding up both hands as
" he approached them) !   Ay, ay, I
" knew well enough, *Edward*, what
" the ſprain in your hand would come
" to.   In truth, my pretty creature
" (applying himſelf to *Maria)* this
" Love may well be called a child of
" the Devil."

" I AM ſorry, Sir (ſhe returned,
" with an arch look), you have reaſon
" to ſay this."

" I WILL more than ſay it (he re-
" plied); I will prove it too; for the
" Devil is the father of lyars; and is
" not at leaſt one half what a lover
                                    " ſays

" fays made up of lyes? Here's *Ed-*
" *ward* could not bowl; no, not he,
" fo violently had he fprained his
" hand; when, was it to be examined,
" I will lay any bett it is as well,
" though not quite fo hard, as my
" own. However, he is an honeft
" fellow; and if he has told you he
" loves you, I will be bound for him
" he faid no more in that than the
" truth. Nay, by my truth, young
" Lady, I cannot help loving you
" myfelf. You are too good and
" too pretty for any body but my *Ed-*
" *ward*."

Miss *Coventry* anfwered him only
by a graceful bow. As for his fon,
he expreffed the gratitude which he
could not avoid feeling in a manner
fo inimitably charming, that, had not
Maria's

Maria's heart been already gone, she could not after this have detained it.

THE sky portending a sudden shower, drove in the other company. The conversation became general; their tea was sipped without scandal; and, soon after, cards were produced; not because agreeable subjects were exhausted, but to make every thing pleasing to Lady *L—*, who had been accustomed to them in the *beau monde*, but never sacrificed either repose or good-humour to the mottled deities.

DAME Fortune so contrived matters for *Edward*, that he and Miss *Coventry* cut out after the first rubber. The latter, retiring to a bow-window at which was chained her squirrel, took up some nuts, and was present-
ing

ing them to the little infenfible from the whiteft hand in the univerfe, when her lover, following the dictates of his paffion, placed himfelf at her elbow, and attempting to take it, his prefumption was punifhed by the teeth of *Maria*'s favourite, which feized on one of his fingers.

" CROSS animal (faid fhe, frown-
" ing) ! go back to thy cell. Was it
" not for my love to thy mafter, thou
" fhouldft be banifhed from my fight.

" A PRESENT from the good Doc-
" tor, I prefume, Madam ? "

" No, Sir."

" PARDON my inquifitivenefs. Your
" father then ? But did Mifs *Coventry*
" get it from abroad ? "

" MY

" MY father has never seen it till
" very lately ; neither can I tell you
" if it is foreign."

" HAPPY giver ! (said he, with a
" sigh, perhaps the deepest that ever
" came from a human heart.)   I see
" my fate; I was not worthy.   I will
" try to bear it with resignation." Saying this, he went back to the card-
table, leaving *Maria* full of astonish-
ment at his words and manner. It
was some minutes before she could re-
collect herself enough to discover to
what it was owing. How, then, did
she blame her indiscretion ? It was too
plain he thought her heart engaged to
the person who had given the squirrel.
Could she undeceive him ? Honour,
gratitude, forbad her. The secret of
Mr. *Gore*, at all events, must not be

VOL. II.   G   given

given up. Her heart was torn by a thoufand - difagreeable imaginations. She would have given the world to have convinced the amiable youth, that it was for him alone fhe had ever felt the leaft partiality.

Tired with her own reflections, fhe rejoined the party, affuming an air of eafe and ferenity which fhe was far from feeling.

Her eyes were the whole night, when unobferved, employed in watching thofe of her beloved *Edward*. What new caufe found fhe there for uneafinefs! Thofe features which ufed to bloom with health and chearfulnefs, were now overclouded, pale, and dejected. His frequent fighs but too plainly told her what he fuffered.

His

His father was extremely concerned at this alteration, which was
viſible to the whole company. He
had no ſurmiſe that it was occaſioned
by Miſs *Coventry :* He plumed himſelf on being a penetrating phyſiogno-
miſt; and had diſcovered, in the
countenance of that lady, no diſlike
to his dear *Edward.* He therefore
credited an excuſe his ſon framed, of
a violent pain in his head, which gave
him a pretence of retiring early to his
chamber; nor, by all his entreaties,
could he prevail on the old gentleman
to leave him till he was in bed, and
had taken ſome ſack-whey.

Poor *Maria* ſtood in little leſs
need of aſſiſtance; eſpecially when,
on his return, he declared great ap-
prehenſions that his *Edward* was

G 2   ſeized

feized with a fever. Every one expreffed
their concern, and tried to comfort
the good father; but their efforts
were ineffectual: He fat with them
but a few minutes; then ftarting from
his chair, " I cannot be eafy (he
" cried) though I have left *Scipio*
" with him. I muft go myfelf, and
" liften at his door. My poor boy!
" My poor dear boy! what would be-
" come of me, fhould I lofe thee!"

" GOOD creature (faid Lord *L*—,
" as he left the room)! Hearts fuch as
" his are invaluable."

" I NEVER faw a face (replied Mr.
" *Coventry*) that bore a truer index of
" the mind. I revere the tender love
" that glows in his honeft breaft for
" this amiable fon."

" How

" " How would your reverence be
" heightened (added Lord *L—*), was
" I to tell you a few of thofe worthy
" generous actions with which I am
" acquainted, but not at liberty to
" reveal."

" My dear (faid Mr. *Coventry*), I
" would have you fend the houfe-
" keeper fometimes to Mr. *Vaughan*'s
" apartment: This black fervant may
" not be ufed to fick people."

MARIA was rifing to obey her father, when his Lordfhip prevented
her, by afluring them *Scipio* was not
only the moft faithful, but the moft
tender creature in the world. " I
" know (continued he) that he will
" never be taxed with neglect or
" negligence where the peace or fafety
" of his mafter are concerned. Once

G 3

" he

" he has faved his life already ; and I
" dare fay would do it a fecond time,
" even at the expence of his own."

HERE Mr. *Vaughan* re-entered,
with the pleafing account that his fon
was much better, and juft compofing
himfelf to fleep ; which gave a mo-
mentary eafe to the wounded heart of
Maria ; though, when fhe retired to
reft, reft flew from her ; and finding
it would be in vain to purfue it, fhe
arofe at five, to put in execution a
fcheme concluded on for fome hours,
of no lefs confequence than a vifit to
the Hermit, whom fhe propofed ac-
quainting with what had happened
the preceding day ; and alfo to requeft
his advice how to extricate herfelf
from the perplexing difficulty into
which fhe had inadvertently plunged.

JUST

JUST as she was stepping to the chariot with these intentions, she saw *Scipio* at the door. She enquired impatiently after his master; and being told by that faithful creature, who had sat up by him the whole night, that he was much better, " Thank God!" said the tender-hearted *Maria*, almost loud enough to be overheard; ordering the coachman to drive as fast as possible, intending to be home again before the family met at breakfast.

HERE I must observe, that since the arrival of their company from *London*, it had been the constant custom of Miss *Coventry* to drive, at least, every other morning to *Combe Woods*. Nothing would she suffer to obstruct this laudable duty of visiting her adopted father, who could only be said to enjoy life when she was with him.—But it is

G 4.   not

not my defign to attend Mifs *Coventry* ;
I fhall therefore go back to that hour,
when the preceding evening Mr. *Edward Vaughan* retired to his apartment,
carrying with him a gueft which never
fails to torment thofe who entertain
him.   Numberlefs are the names he
goes by. *Shakefpeare* calls him " green-
" eyed monfter:" but I think with
more propriety he might have been
term'd a " pelican," as he is fure to
feed on thofe from whom he draws
his exiftence.

Scipio, almoft diftracted to fee his
beloved mafter devoured with grief,
entreated, begged even with tears, to
. know the caufe. " Indeed,   my
" *Mafar*, your poor *Scipio* die (faid
" the honeft creature) if you no
" tell him. He fee you be very bad
" in your dear heart, or you no
" figh

" figh fo.—Folks in my country do
" juft fo, when de be in love. Hea-
" ven preferve my *Mafar* from
" being in love."

" WHY, *Scipio* (replied Mr. *Vaughan*),
" is there any thing fo very dreadful
" in that paffion, that makes you pray
" fo heartily againft it? Was you ever
" in love?"

" O YES, my *Mafar*, many, many
" time; but not wit your colour.—
" Your colour be bad colour, *Mafar*;
" your women be bad women."

" You have feen but few of them yet,
" *Scipio*; but can the moft beautiful of
" your Tawneys compare with the mif-
" trefs of this houfe? Her eyes, her teeth,
" her lips, for colour they may equal;

G 5 " but

" but can they fhew fuch fymmetry of
" features! fuch a fhape!"

" Ah *Mafar*, *Mafar*! (fhaking his
" head) me fee now what be de mat-
" ter:—You look, you do look, my
" *Mafar*, juft as poor *Pompey* look be-
" fore he hang himfelf."

" What tempted him, my good
" creature, to commit fo rafh an ac-
" tion?"

" Pompey love *Phebe*; *Phebe* no
" love *Pompey*: fo *Pompey* cry—*Pom-*
" *pey* howl;—but ftill no *Phebe* love
" him:—fo ten, my *Mafar*, after he
" cry and howl again, he hang himfelf
" becaufe *Phebe* no love him."

" Well

"WELL but, *Scipio*, ſuppoſe I
"ſhould be in love, why is my caſe ſo
"deſperate as *Pompey's?"*

"O ᴍʏ *Maſar*, your miſtreſs no
"kind,—no kind to you!—ſhe no
"love you :—ſhe love anoder."

"Aʜ *Scipio*, what is it you ſay?"

"Mᴇ ſay, my *Maſar*, your ſweet-
"heart meet man in de trees,—in de
"woods.—*Dick* drives her in de
"coach to de trees—to de woods—to
"meet man."

"Aɴᴅ did *Dick* tell you this? I
"was but half miſerable before! What
"man does Miſs *Coventry* meet?—In
"what woods does ſhe meet him?

"Nᴀʏ,

" NAY, my *Mafar*, me know :—
" *Dick* know noting that fhe do meet
" man. *Dick* fay he tink fhe meet
" man. *Dick* fay her airing to de
" trees—to de woods—be not for no-
" ting."

THIS laft fpeech of honeft *Scipio*
eafed his mafter's heart from part of
its intolerable load; yet ftill he afked
with impatience, " What airings do
" you talk of ? She has taken none fince
" my arrival ?"

" AH *Mafar*, you know no matter !
" Your love be gone and home again
" before you be up in de morn."

" BUT you have not told me to
" what woods fhe is carried ? Good
" *Scipio*, if thou knoweft, tell me
" quickly."

" ME

" ME would tell *Mafar*, did me
" know. *Dick* be a beaſt : *Dick* no
" tell me."

" WHAT do you mean by a
" beaſt?"

" HE put de glaſs to his mouth ;
" he take it away : he put it to his
" mouth, and take it away ſo many
" times, he could no put there any
" more :—ſo he fall all along, and
" four white men carried him to bed.
" Was he no beaſt, *Mafar*?"

" A BEAST, indeed! But has he
" never told you any more about his
" Lady?"

" No more, no more, *Mafar*:
" *Dick* never be the beaſt ſince."

MR.

MR. *Vaughan*, who would have laughed heartily at any other time, was now abforbed in melancholy reflections, and could not help exclaiming, " Why did I return to my native land ! " I ought to have known before, from " dreadful experience, that to me, at " leaft, it could produce nothing but " misfortunes." Then turning to *Scipio*, " Could you not contrive (faid " he) for me to fpeak to *Dick?*"— Again reflecting a moment, " No, I " will not fpeak to him. Why fhould " I bribe him to betray the fecrets of " his Lady? Yet thefe heart-rending " airings! I muft, I will know what " thy mean. On you, my good " *Scipio*, I can depend. Follow her " carriage ; but follow it at a diftance. " Your feet are as fwift as thofe of " the fleeteft horfe ; watch well the " motions of my Love: Yet be cau-
" tious

" tious that neither she or any of her
" attendants may difcover thee. Even
" a certainty, my good creature, that
" she loves another man better than
" thy mafter, cannot make him more
" unhappy than that dreadful fufpence
" to which he is now reduced."

" BE there de ting under de blue
" heaven (replied the kind foul) that
" I no do for ferve my dear *Mafar?*
" Have me no left my own world,
" my fater, my moter, to follow you
" to yours? Now, my *Mafar*, should
" you go to de world farther tan this,
" me go too, if a you promife they no
" make me a white man. You once
" tell a me, *Mafar*, when we come
" there, we be all changed: now me
" don't chufe to be oter colour."

" GOOD

" GOOD creature ! thy virtues will
" there shine brighter (replied Mr.
" *Vaughan*) than diamonds would here
" on thy jetty skin." At the same time
holding out his hand, *Scipio* fell
upon his knees, kissing it with a reverence and ardour which I fear
some of us cannot be said to feel
when we prostrate ourselves before
the Lord of the universe.

AFTER this conversation Mr.
Vaughan pretended to fall asleep, partly
that he might be at liberty to indulge
his own reflections, and partly to quiet
the mind of his faithful *Scipio*;
though, if he had found any inclination
of that kind, it would have been im-
possible to have indulged it, as his care-
ful attendant every five or six minutes
opened the curtains, and held a candle
to his face: at other times he would
lay

lay his ear to the mouth of his mafter, to difcover if he breathed. Thefe were his conftant employments till the day broke, when going to the window he faw the chariot drive round to the front door, he left the room with caution: and was at the door before Mifs *Coventry.* Her tender enquiries for his mafter almoft convinced *Scipio Dick*'s conjectures were ill founded. Hoping to find this really the cafe, he fet out with alacrity, following the track of her chariot, never once coming near enough to be feen.

It ftopped at the ufual place. Mifs *Coventry* alighted, and with a quick ftep croffed the little Common. A brake which led to the wood brought him to the fame fpot, though by a different way. He followed her unperceived. When fhe ftopped at the
Rock,

Rock, *Scipio* was concealed behind a
large clump of trees; but his fur-
prize was fo great that he was in danger of difcovering himfelf, when Mifs
Coventry opened the little door which
led into the Rock, fhut it after her,
and difappeared in an inftant.

THE Black, who had no notion
that there could be a door in that
place, really imagined he had feen
the Rock open and fwallow her up;
and fearing to ftay, left the fame fate
might attend him, he once more took
to his heels, meafuring back his fteps
with fo much eager fpeed, that he
was almoft fainting when he entered
his mafter's chamber.

SUCH a ghaftly figure could not
again be exhibited: Eyes ftaring, or
rather rolling; hands extended; nofe
                                    ftretched

ftretched to an enormous breadth;
add to this, his whole perfon not drop-
ping, but ftreaming with fweat.

" Good Heavens (faid Mr. *Vaughan*)!
" what can have fo greatly difcom-
" pofed thee?"

" Oh *Mafar*, *Mafar* (cried the af-
" frighted creature)! Great chance
" you ever fee poor *Scipio* more.
" Rocks do no fo in my country. Ah
" poor miftrefs! you fafe enough;
" you no come out again to plague
" my *Mafar*."

" What do you mean, *Scipio?*
" What am I to underftand? Thou
" art certainly bereft of thy fenfes.
" Leave this nonfenfe. Did Mifs *Co-*
" *ventry* go out to-day? Did you do

" as

" as I defired? Did fhe meet any
" perfon? Is fhe returned?"

" ME no come out of dat wall,
" *Mafar*, if me be faftened in; tell a
" me, *Mafar*?"

" WHY that queftion (cried Mr.
" *Vaughan*, a little peevifhly)? Thou
" putteft my patience to a fevere trial.

" WHY then, my *Mafar*, if me no
" come out of dat wall, your miftrefs
" no come out of de rock. Me fware
" by de moon, me faw de rock fwal-
" low your miftrefs."

" GOOD God! *Scipio*, what can I
" make of all this? It is impoffible to
" be as thou haft faid, and you are
" too honeft to impofe a falfhood on
" me.

" me. This affair is extremely un-
" accountable; but it cannot be as you
" apprehend. Ah! fee, the chariot
" is returned, and Mifs *Coventry* alight-
" ing from it."

Scipio would not be convinced that
it was really her, but owned there was
a great likenefs : " No, no (cried the
" faithful creature); dat be no *Ma-*
" *far*'s miftrefs; dat be bad fpirit.
" *Mafar*'s miftrefs be very fure in de
" rock."

Mr. *Vaughan* knew not what to
make of the intelligence brought him
by *Scipio*; neither could he guefs by
what accident his fenfes had been fo
ftrongly impofed upon; therefore determined himfelf to find out the bottom of this myfterious affair.

En-

ENJOINING *Scipio* to fecrecy, he told him that he would go and fee this dreadful rock, of which he reported fuch wonders : " But it muft " be (faid he), when Mifs *Coventry* " again takes that road ; and be fure " get out of your friend *Dick* the " next time fhe orders the chariot, as " it will be neceffary for us to fet out " fomething earlier, that we may con- " ceal ourfelves and horfes before fhe " arrives."

To this *Scipio* would not for a long while confent ; nothing but an abfolute command could have prevailed on him to carry his beloved mafter to the horrible place of which he had fuch dread.

CHAP.

CHAP. XIX.

THE entrance of the elder Mr.
Vaughan broke off this conversation. Not that I would have my
readers suppose it was the first visit his
father had made him that morning;
anxious fears for the health of *Edward* had awaked him before his usual
hour; but finding the invalid better
than he expected, he told him he would
take a walk in those beautiful planta-
tions with which this house was sur-
rounded.

MR. *Vaughan* was now returned
from that walk, intending to propose
something to his son which he thought

could

could not fail of giving him pleafure.
Scipio, who was by this time tolera-
bly recovered from his fright, left
the room as foon as his old mafter
entered.

" I HOPE, dear Sir (faid *Ed-*
" *ward*, who was juft dreffed), you
" have been agreeably entertained in
" your little excurfion."

" FAITH (replied he), it is a no-
" ble place, boy; but not half fo no-
" ble as the poffeffor. *Coventry* has a
" good heart, and would be an ex-
" cellent companion if he was not
" quite fo low-fpirited."

" AND yet I know your heart fo
" well, my dear father (returned the
" other), that I am fure you honour
" him for this very difpofition. Ah,
" Sir !

" Sir ! had you or I loſt ſuch a
" wife——"

" WHY that's true, *Ned*; I confeſs
" it a heavy misfortune. Faith, *Maria*
" is a ſweet girl ; they ſay, the very
" picture of her mother."

" MARIA, Sir ! *Maria !*"

" OH ho, young man ! what, does
" her name raiſe your colour, and can't
" you ſpeak it without heſitation ? I
" thought as much yeſterday; I hint-
" ed as much, you know. I am ſel-
" dom out in theſe matters. And,
" for your comfort, my boy, I can ſee
" the little cherub has no diſlike to
" you."

A PROFOUND ſigh, which iſſued
from the breaſt of *Edward*, ſpoke he

VOL. II.   H   was

was not of his father's opinion; who
thus continued:

" THIS very morning I'll propofe
" the affair, by the Lord *Harry!* I
" have no notion of ftanding fhilly-
" fhally, when both are willing. My
" fortune fhall be all your own; I'll
" lay it before *Coventry*; he fhall take
" every farthing, if he will but confent
" to make my dear child happy."

" MY more than father! your
" goodnefs, your generofity oppreffes
" me. But, deareft, dear Sir, though
" I own I love Mifs *Coventry*, yet, for
" feveral reafons, I muft beg you will
" not fpeak on this occafion, either
" to the lady or her father, for fome
" days. As to your kind, generous
" intentions, how fhall I find words to
" thank you?"

" I HATE

" I HATE words. Your miftrefs,
" my boy (with a fmile), may like
" them better. However, fince you
" defire it, I will wait one week be-
" fore I fay any thing of this matter :
" though, by *Jove*, I cannot think
" for what reafon. When I was at
" your years, had fuch a pretty girl
" been in the cafe, I fhould have de-
" fired no *put-offs*."

HERE a fummons to breakfaft
haftened them down ftairs, where
they found the company all met, and
the elegant, the charming Mifs *Coventry* feated at the tea-table: I cannot
fay blooming and rofy as the morning;
Grief, the preceding night, had with
her malignant finger touched the
queen of flowers; or, to fpeak more
plain, the colour on *Maria*'s cheeks

had given place to an alarming pale-
nefs; at which change none felt greater
uneafinefs than *Edward*. When her
friends expreffed their concern for her
health, fhe affured them it was never
better. " I have been up (faid fhe)
" more than four hours, and have
" had a delightful airing: my dear
" father is fond of my ufing exer-
" cife."

The words " delightful airing"
brought fo much colour into the face
of *Edward*, that, to hide his confufion,
he was obliged to leave his chair, and
go to the window.

" Had you mentioned your inten-
" tions laft night, (faid Mifs *Haftings)*
" I would gladly have been of your
" party.—I approve of early rifing:—
" though

" though it is but feldom that I can
" mufter up refolution enough to put
" it into practice."

A conversation was now introduced very agreeable to thofe who
like to behold the infant beauties of
the Morning ; but as I apprehend few
of my readers ever fee *Aurora* but in
a more advanced ftate, I fhall for that
reafon omit it, to acquaint them the
Hermit had by his fine fenfe and phi-
lofophical arguments convinced his
dear daughter, as he now always
called Mifs *Coventry*, that " whatever
" is, is beft." " My child (faid he),
" as you have defcribed this young
" man, he appears worthy your ten-
" dereft regard. There is but one
" thing in his difpofition I would wifh
" otherwife.—Jealoufy, my Love, of
" all the deftructive paffions, is that

　　　　" which

" which threatens the greateſt miſery
" to its poſſeſſor.—I do not ſay but it
" will ſometimes take root in minds
" the moſt perfect: in the richeſt
" ground are often found the moſt
" luxuriant weeds: but from ſuch a
" ſoil reaſon can quickly eradicate them.
" You aſk my advice how to act.—
" Your own good ſenſe, my dear, will
" dictate better than it is poſſible for
" me to adviſe :—Yet as you ſtate the
" matter, I think it abſolutely neceſſary
" that if you can come to an eclairciſſe-
" ment with any propriety, you ſhould
" ſatisfy the young gentleman that the
" perſon who gave you the little animal
" which has occaſioned both ſuch diſ-
" quiet, is a poor old man, who has
" been toſſed to and fro on the waves
" of Misfortune, and at length eſcap-
" ing the rough rocks againſt which
" they have ſo often daſhed him, has
" crept

" crept from the world to this hidden
" corner, where he waits his final diffo-
" lution.—For your and his happinefs
" (continued he), I confent you fhall
" reveal my fecret:—but under the
" fame reftrictions on which it was dif-
" covered to yourfelf.—If my dear
" daughter approves of this plan, let
" me fee her as foon as fhe has put it
" into execution."

MARIA with a thoufand acknowledgements embraced the good man's
propofal. She promifed all he afked,
and returned to *Hartly-row* with a
mind more at eafe by the hope that it
was now in her power to convince
Edward his fufpicions were without
foundation.

ALL that day paffed, and fhe found
not the opportunity fhe fo much wifhed

H 4   for.

for. Inftead of feeking to engage, he feemed ftudioufly to avoid her. The following was equally unpropitious. A thoufand times he was about to throw himfelf at her feet; but a facred power feemed to with-hold him.

How impatiently did he wait till the next night, when, on going to his chamber, *Scipio* acquainted him that *Dick* had received his lady's orders to get ready at fix in the morning.

This intelligence drove fleep from the eyes of Mr. *Vaughan*, and the hours between twelve and five feemed an age; for uncertainty is doubtlefs the moft unweary of all fituations.

At length appeared the much wifhed-for dawn, and *Scipio*, not like the

the Sun unlefs in an eclipfe, entered
the room.

WHILST affifting his mafter to drefs,
he ufed a thoufand prayers and entreaties that he would not go to the Wood.
" I can't for my life (faid Mr. *Vaughan*)
" think what whim, my good creature,
" has entered thy head; but prithee
" fay no more to diffuade me: I am
" refolved to fee this wonderful Rock.
" Yet, at the fame time, to quiet thy
" honeft fears about me, I promife
" not to venture near it, if I fee the leaft
" appearance of danger."

SOMEWHAT fatisfied with this affu-
rance, he conducted his mafter, though
not unreluctantly, to thofe trees which
had concealed him on his firft excurfion.

H 5   " I SHOULD

"I should think this place (faid
"Mr. *Vaughan*)inchantingly beautiful,
"if it did not occur to me that here
"the moft charming of her fex makes
"happy with her prefence fome fa-
"voured lover. Yet perhaps I wrong
"her:—May fhe not pafs thofe hours
"in pleafing contemplation!—Thefe
"woods feem calculated to infpire
"them.—Befides, does not her un-
"fpotted reputation—her delicacy—
"that duty—that reverence—fhe pays
"the beft of parents,—all declare that
"fhe would not receive the private ad-
"dreffes of any man?—Why had I
"not fooner made thefe reflections
"(continued he)? Certainly my doubts
"were groundlefs. What muft fhe
"think of my late behaviour?"

WHILST his mafter was indulging
thefe cogitations, *Scipio* had fixed his
eyes

eyes on that place which he fo much dreaded, expecting every moment to fee it again open; expectations by which he was fo greatly terrified, that his woolly hair gradually uncurled, and at laft ftood almoft erect: nor did his fears receive any fmall addition from the fudden appearance of Mifs *Coventry*, who was entered the narrow path, and with nimble fteps fpeeded towards the Rock.

At this fight he was going to roar out; but his mafter, who had alfo feen her, forbad him, on the forfeiture of his love.

This was enough: he would have been mute, though a knife had been held at his throat: he only fell on his knees, and fqueezing the hand of Mr. *Vaughan*, in a whifper begged he

H 6 would

would not be deluded by that evil fpirit. But alas! his mafter was incapa-
ble of anfwering him; his jealoufy,
like a torrent, was returned, rufhing
on him with fuch rapidity, that it almoft bore away his fenfes.

The poor Black, who was ftill on
his knees, had not feen what raifed his
mafter to a degree of frenzy.

" Scipio, (faid he with eyes flafhing
" fire) if you love me, if you value
" my eternal peace, if you wifh not to
" fee me miferable the reft of my days,
" —attempt not to follow me;—move
" not a ftep from this fpot till I return.
" —Should you difobey me, this is
" the laft day we live together."

He did not wait for an anfwer, but
flew to the Rock, and felt joy, if his
bofom

bofom could now be faid to harbour
fuch a gueft, when he faw the door
ftill open; Mifs *Coventry* neglecting
a thing fhe had never done before, to
fhut it on the infide.

THOUGHT is not fwifter than were
the fteps of *Edward* till he reached the
bottom of the Cavern.—There he
ftopped, and thus argued with himfelf:
—" By what right do I enter this dark
" abode ?—Why fhould I by my pre-
" fence interrupt their ftolen inter-
" views?—Without a doubt fhe loves
" my happy rival.—That hand which
" I faw her receive with fuch tranf-
" port,—nay kifs it, if my eyes deceived
" me not;—that hand muft and ought
" to be the hand to which her's fhould
" be united. Adieu, thou fallen an-
" gel!" continued he; and was juft
going

going to return : but hearing Mifs *Coventry* pronounce the name of *Vaughan*, and a voice which thrilled through his very foul repeat it emphatically, he rufhed forward, entered the cave, and throwing himfelf on the neck of the Hermit, fomething that bore fo near a refemblance to death as might have been eafily miftaken for it, took from him the power of fpeech : he could only cry out "My father!" At the fame inftant, the old man giving a violent fcream, both fell lifelefs to the ground.

Good God ! what a fight for Mifs *Coventry!* It almoft bereft her of her fenfes.—She tried to difunite the arms of her beloved *Edward* from the neck of her adopted father; but Death's younger brother rendered all her efforts

forts ineffectual.—She applied her eau-de-luce first to one, then to the other.

WHAT would she have given for the affistance of honeft *Simon* and *Betty*; but she knew not the dark meandering path that led to their abode.—The next people who prefented themfelves to her affrighted imagination, were her own fervants; and to thefe she fled.

HER love, her terror, her concern, had transformed her to a fecond *Mercury*. To have feen her, you muft have thought wings had fupplied the place of feet.

ALREADY had she fkimmed the Woods, and was alighted on the Common, when three or four horfemen came

came full fpeed towards her. Their appearance at any other time would have filled her breaft with apprehenfions, but had now a quite different effect.

STEPPING up to the firft without looking in his face, " I beg for hea-" ven's fake, Sir, (faid fhe) if you have " the leaft compaffion——"

" GOOD God! my child!" interrupted Mr. *Coventry*, difmounting, and catching her in his paternal arms: " What alarms you thus? What has " brought you to this place unat-" tended?"

SHE had not time to anfwer, *Scipio* at that inftant feizing her by the arm, fwearing by the fun, moon, and ftars, fhe was an evil fpirit, and fhould not live

live another minute, if she did not produce his dear *Masar*.

THE distracted *Maria* was freed
from his paw by her father and Mr.
Vaughan, the latter begging she would
pardon the honest fellow's frenzy.
" *Scipio* thinks (said he) that you have
" kidnapped my son. He has told us
" strange tales of a rock that swallows
" up every one who comes near it: He
" has sworn that he saw you and my
" *Edward* closed in it. Though we
" gave no attention to his idle story,
" we were obliged, unless we would
" see him put an end to his life, to
" follow him hither."

" I CAN account for what the good
" creature has told you (said Miss *Co-*
" *ventry*), but have not time now for
" an explanation. Follow my steps,
" " if

" if you hope ever again to fee that
" perfon you call your fon:" Saying
which fhe fpeeded her fteps towards
the Cave, which fhe entered fo pre-
cipitately, that they had not time to afk
any queftions.

THE Hermit recovered in the abfence of *Maria*, and was now leaning
over the body of *Edward*, his eyes
rivetted on his ftill lifelefs face, the big
tears falling on it in fuch abundance as
plainly fhewed it was not in the power
of water to recover him.

SCIPIO rufhed in after Mifs *Coventry:*
the fears for his mafter having got the
better of thofe for his own life, he
paid no attention to any other object.——
Springing forwards, he caught him in
his arms,——and in fpite of all re-
fiftance ran with him into the air,
where

where laying him on the grafs, he began to fhew fome figns of returning life.

No fooner had the worthy creature performed this kind office, than he was obliged to give place to two who preffed forwards, both calling themfelves the fathers of their dear, their beloved, and one of his reftored fon.

Now followed fuch a fcene as my pen cannot defcribe. Mr. *Vaughan*, who the Hermit at firft fight recollected to be that kind, that generous friend with whom his darling *Edward* had left *England*, now again reftored the noble, the deferving youth to his arms. —How did he ftrain by turns to his grateful bofom his friend, and that
dear

dear son he had so long thought dead.

FOR a long time nothing was to be heard but broken interrupted sentences. The joy they felt knew no bounds; it would not admit of method: it was more than an hour before it began to subside; though in that time Miss *Coventry* and her father partook of their caresses. Nor was the good *Scipio* forgot: his happiness was supreme. To see his master restored to life and to his parent, filled his honest soul with tumultuous gladness, which shewed itself in a thousand antick motions.—He skipped to and fro like one possessed, kissing the hands of this truly happy company, which they obligingly extended for that purpose; nor could he avoid repeating his salute

on

on the charming hand of *Maria*. He
was now intirely reconciled to that
young Lady, and abfolutely convinced
of her being flefh and blood. Mr.
Coventry, in order to calm this fudden
guft of tranfport in his faithful breaft,
begged he would return to *Hartly-row*,
and fend Lord *L*——'s coach to the
Wood immediately; "For I cannot
" confent, Sir (fpeaking to Mr. *Gore*),
" that you fhall ever again return to
" your gloomy habitation. My daugh-
" ter, whilft you was giving vent to pa-
" rental rapture, has told me the heads
" of your hitherto melancholy ftory."

"INDEED, indeed, my dear Sir,
" (faid *Maria*) you muft oblige my
" father: let your adopted daugh-
" ter prevail. Can you, will you refufe
" her?"

" HE

"He muſt, he ſhall (ſaid Mr.
"Vaughan, taking his hand). What
"does my friend think?—Is not five
"years enough to have been buried?
"Beſides, Edward ſhall not again loſe
"his father."

"Allow me, my ſecond parent, to
"declare (ſaid the graceful youth) that
"if my moſt revered and beloved fa-
"ther will not quit this cell, I alſo
"muſt make it the place of my
"abode."

"That you ſhall not (returned Mr.
"Gore); I cannot refuſe my child, my
"friends. Though I had determined
"never more to appear in the world, yet
"it was thy ſuppoſed death, my dear
"Edward, which occaſioned that de-
"termination; and ſince Heaven has re-
"ſtored, thec ſo unexpectedly, let my
                              "grateful

" grateful thanks to the Almighty be
" poured out before thoufands and
" ten thoufands of his people! But
" why, why, my generous good friend
" (to Mr. *Vaughan*), did you not be-
" fore acquaint me with the joyful
" tidings?"

" I CERTAINLY fhould have done
" it (returned he), if you had given
" me a direction to this your country-
" feat."

" I SEE it is only myfelf that am
" to blame (he replied). I have all
" my life been in purfuit of Happi-
" nefs; but it has hitherto fleeted
" from my grafp. I fought it in con-
" cealment; but now find, to have
" met it I muft have continued in the
" world. Again it appears; it holds
                                    " out

" out its extended arms: Yet thofe
" embraces it is about to give will
" not, I fear, be lafting, unlefs—un-
" lefs—but I cannot fpeak.   What a
" prefumption!"

" I AM glad of it (faid Mr.
" *Vaughan*), as I have had an inten-
" tion to do it all this morning.   But
" perhaps what we have to fay may
" be on very different fubjects: Mine,
" I freely own, is on the good old fub-
" ject, matrimony."

THEY fmiled, and he continued:

" You muft know, Sir (to Mr. *Co-*
" *ventry*), I have threefcore thoufand
" pounds, which I intend to beftow
" on your charming daughter, if you
" confent, Sir.——This is the hand
" that

" that muſt preſent it (taking Mr.
" *Edward Gore*'s.) Join it, my friend,
" with that of your amiable *Maria*."

" Too much! too much, Sir (ex-
" claimed Mr. *Gore*)! This is too
" much! God Almighty preſerve my
" ſenſes!" He went from the company; whilſt *Edward*, on a bended
knee, bathed the hand of his truly-
generous benefactor with tears of
gratitude.

Mr. *Coventry* was loſt in admiration: He could not reply till a ſecond
time called on by Mr. *Vaughan*. When
he did, it completed the happineſs of
all: He declared, if his daughter had
no objection, not another event could
give him equal ſatisfaction.

"Let me entreat, my deareſt Miſs
"Coventry (ſaid the perſuaſive Ed-
"ward, his face glowing with love),
"that you will not render me miſera-
"ble, juſt as I have drank ſo very
"deep of felicity."

"Come, come, my cherub (added
"Mr. Vaughan), you cannot be cruel
"to my dear boy. By my troth, had
"I been a pretty young lady, I think
"I ſhould have had him at the firſt
"word.   But tell us at once, will you
"give Ned your heart? or will you,
"by your refuſal, old and tough as it
"is, break mine?"

"I cannot grant what you aſk,
"Sir (ſaid Miſs Coventry); that heart
"you ſo partially ſolicit is already diſ-
"poſed of."

"Zounds!

" Zounds! not grant it? not have
" my boy (cried Mr. *Vaughan*, ſtamp-
" ing up and down)? Here's a fine
" piece of work at laſt! What, after
" ſmiling on him ſo like an angel, and
" now ſay you have not a heart to
" give him, with a duce!"

" Pray, Sir (ſaid Miſs *Coventry*),
" let not you and I quarrel;" holding
out her lilly hand, with ineffable
ſweetneſs. But the old gentleman,
inſtead of taking it, put both his behind him.

" No, no, I am not to be wheedled
" ſo, young Lady. Not give *Ned* your
" heart!"

" Pardon me, Sir; you miſtook
" my words. I ſaid my heart was
" beſtowed; but did I ſay it was not

" in the poſſeſſion of your adopted
" ſon ?"

" HEAVENLY goodneſs (ſaid the
" enraptured *Edward) !* Sure I have
" never, never been unhappy ! O my
" lovely creature, repeat theſe words !
" Repeat them every hour, that I
" may not think them an illuſion.

" My daughter, you know not (ſaid
" Mr. *Coventry)* how happy you make
" me, by giving hopes that I ſhall call
" this amiable youth my ſon."

" Now all is as it ſhould be (added
" Mr. *Vaughan)*. She is more than
" ever my cherub ! my pink ! my
" roſe ! Come, let me once more
" (taking her hand) ſee that lilly you
" juſt now held out to me. How
" ſoft ! how ſmooth ! By the Lord
Harry,

" *Harry*, I muſt give it one kiſs!——
" But where is our friend (continued
" he)? I'll lay any wager, *Ned*, thy
" father has again buried himſelf.
" Prithee, ferret him out. I am al-
" moſt as much afraid to enter that
" place as honeſt *Scipio*. But ſee, he
" comes: Look at his eyes; they ſhew
" how much his worthy heart has
" been affeeted."

EDWARD flew to meet his parent,
to acquaint him of his happineſs, and
to conduct him to his expecting
friends. What pleaſure did theſe
tidings give him! He folded to his
breaſt his deareſt daughter; he wept
over her; whilſt her gentle boſom
could ſcarce contain the joy it felt. To
his noble generous friend he would
have ſpoke; but a weight of obligations choaked his words.

I 3   MR.

MR. *Vaughan* faw his diftrefs; and, to relieve it, expreffed an aftonifhment that Mr. *Gore* had fhewn no curiofity to know by what miracle his fon was ftill alive.

"AH, my friend (he replied), my
"*Edward* lives! Is not that enough
"for me to know?"

"YET, pray tell us (faid *Maria*)
"by what means you efcaped the
"dreadful flames."

EDWARD returned a graceful bow to his fair miftrefs, and proceeded thus.

"THE fire in our veffel, occafioned
"by the careleffnefs of a boy, burnt
"with fuch fury that we foon found
"all our efforts to extinguifh it were
"ineffectual. I cannot paint the me-
"lancholy

" lancholy fcene. Every one gave
" himfelf up for death, which ap-
" peared unavoidable. Some of my
" friends, hoping to efcape, threw
" themfelves into the water; but their
" hopes were baffled. I had the af-
" fliction to fee them perifh; yet, fur-
" rounded by the mercilefs flames, I
" was juft going to follow their ex-
" ample, when I faw fomething fwim-
" ming towards the fhip. I might
" have miftaken it for the buoy of
" a veffel, had it not roared out my
" name. Being come clofe to the
" fide, my faithful *Scipio*, for it was
" him, jumped on board; and, with-
" out faying more than " Me no fear,
" *Mafar*," faftened my arms round
" his neck, plunged into the fea, and
" carried me fafe to the fhore.

" I will not repeat the acknowledg-
" ments I made to the preserver of
" my life; but proceed to that mo-
" ment when I threw myself at the
" feet of this best of men.   Our joy
" at this meeting had in it an alloy.
" How unlucky that the ship in which
" the account of my death had been
" hastily transmitted to my father was
" already sailed, and no possibility of
" recalling the unfortunate letter !
" We wrote continually for twelve
" months; but, at the end of the pe-
" riod, received the dreadful account
" of my father's decease.   What have
" I to add ?   Only this; that, at the
" request of my now only friend, I
" took his name, promising not to say
" to any person living but that I was
" his real son."

" Yes

"Yes (interrupted Mr. *Vaughan*,) I
"rather chofe to let him pafs for my
"natural fon, than that his undeferv-
"ing uncle fhould be honoured with
"fuch a nephew."

Scipio now came fkipping forwards
to inform them the coach waited, and
was again careffed in the warmeft
manner, particularly by *Maria*, who
faid to the elder Mr. *Gore*, as they proceeded to their carriage, "Will not ho-
"neft *Simon* and *Betty*, Sir, be a-
"larmed at your abfence?"

"My dear child (he replied), how
"confiderate are you! I have told the
"good fouls what happinefs this day
"has brought me. God be thanked!
"God be thanked! faid 'they, and
"down they dropped on their knees.
"I joined in their pious gratitude: we
praifed

" praifed the Almighty for his mercies,
" and I returned with a heart lefs op-
" preffed than when I left you."

THEY were now come to the verge
of the wood, where the coach and chariot waited. Mr. *Vaughan* and Mr. *Gore*
went in the latter, pulling up the glaffes
as they paffed through *Wheatly*, as Mr.
Gore's long beard might otherwife
have drawn the attention of the mul-
titude.

WHEN they arrived at *Hartly-row*,
both Mr. *Gores* retired to a different room
from the company, where the reve-
rend beard of the now no longer Hermit was fhorn by the mercilefs hand of
a barber, which wrought fuch an alteration on his perfon, that when he
obeyed the breakfaft-fummons, Mifs
Coventry had not the leaft idea of her
adopted

adopted father, the lofs of his beard having taken off at leaft the appearance of twenty years from his age.

MR. *Coventry* introduced him to Lord and Lady *L*——, Mifs *Haftings*, Mr. *Stormont* and Dr. *Edgcome*; each ftriving to outvie the other in expreffions of admiration and efteem : but it was not alone confined to him ; Mr. *Vaughan* and the amiable *Edward* had their fhare.

MARIA, whilft the elder Mr. *Gore* dreffed, had related not only the transactions of that morning, but alfo told them their firft meeting in *Combe Woods*, and his reafons for retiring to that place.

THREE weeks after this memorable day was the time infifted on by Mr. *Vaughan*

Vaughan for uniting the hands of *Edward* and *Maria*; Lord and Lady *L——* confenting to lengthen their vifit, and to grace the nuptials with their prefence.

MISS *Haflings*, at the intreaties of her lover, and the requeft of her noble relations, promifed to beftow her hand at the fame time. In the intermediate fpace they partook of every amufement the country afforded : but none gave them higher pleafure than their frequent excurfions to *Combe Woods*, on which occafions *Simon* and *Betty* were their caterers.

AT length the day arrived in which the happinefs of *Edward* and Mr. *Stormont* was completed by doctor *Edgcome*.—On their return from the church, an elegant chariot paffed them.

them.—It drove too swift to difcover who were in it:—but what an a-greeable furprife to Mrs. *Gore*, to be embraced on alighting by her *Lavinia*.

HERE was a new fource for joy. Mr. *Harry Gore* had, at firft, no re-collection of his uncle; but being in-formed of what had happened in his abfence, he flew into the arms of *Ed-ward*, embracing him with the warmth of an affectionate brother.

I SHALL now only fay, none could feel more real, more exquifite happi-nefs than this little circle. Lord and Lady *L———*, though with infinite re-gret, and not till they had got a pro-mife from the two Mr. *Gores* to bring their Ladies to town the next winter, returned to *London*, as did Mr. and Mrs. *Stormont*.

HERE

HERE I fhould have concluded this
Work ; but thinking my Readers may
be defirous to know fomething more of
Sir *Francis*, I am fortunately enabled
to fatisfy their curiofity.

THE Baronet finding no perfuafions,
no intreaties could gain him the heart
of his fair neighbour, fet out poft for
Millbridge, determined to vent his
fpleen and ill-nature on *Lavinia :* but
he arrived too late ; his fifter was now
the property of a man who would
not fuffer her to be treated with in-
dignity.

SORELY difappointed in the low
fpite he meditated, and ftill in
hopes to vex fomebody, he fet out
for *France*, in company with his old
friend and companion Sir *William
More*, to whom he found means to

be

be eafily reconciled. Lady *Gilford*,
at firft, took his going much to heart,
and laid the intire blame on her fifter
and daughter: but they found a method to moderate his anger; and about
fix months fince her darling returned,
immenfely improved, in the opinion of
the two Mifs *Jones's*.

WITH thefe young Ladies he fpent
the greateft part of his time, which
occafioned no fmall bickerings between
the two candidates: but as Sir *Francis*
happened to be the returning officer,
he declared Mifs *Jones* duly elected,
and fhe took her feat at the *Grange*
accordingly.

POOR Mifs *Patty* would not have
outlived this difappointment, if Sir
William More had not offered himfelf
the very next day.——She was not long
considering:

considering : his title was as good as Sir *Francis's*, his estate better, and in two months Lady *More* was allowed by all the village to have much finer jewels than Lady *Gilford :* but this made not the least uneasiness between the sisters. Their husbands also live in the strict-est unity :—quite a family-compact. Sir *William* is the *cicisbeo* of Lady *Gilford*, whilst Sir *Francis* returns those obligations by his civility to Lady *More.* But I shall pursue this subject no farther, determined not to dip my pen in the treble jetty ink of scandal.

I NOW take leave of my Readers, wishing every married pair may be as happy as were *Edward* and his *Maria*, or *Harry* and his *Lavinia*.

F I N I S.